Praise for Kate Hoffmann
from *RT Book Reviews*…

"Hoffmann's deeply felt, emotional story is riveting.
It's impossible to put down."
— on *The Charmer*

"Fully developed characters and perfect pacing make
this story feel completely right."
— on *Your Bed or Mine?*

"Sexy and wildly romantic."
— on *Doing Ireland!*

"A very hot story mixes with great characters
to make every page a delight."
— on *The Mighty Quinns: Ian*

"Romantic, sexy and heartwarming."
— on *Who Needs Mistletoe?*

"Sexy, heartwarming and romantic…a story to settle
down with and enjoy—and then re-read."
— on *The Mighty Quinns: Teague*

D0487374

Dear Reader,

I can't believe another Quinn saga is coming to an end. *The Mighty Quinns: Ronan* is the fourth and final book about the Seattle branch of the Quinn family and marks my eighteenth Quinn book.

Will I be writing more? Of course! I've already begun planning for the next set of Quinns. I'm going to switch things up a bit and there will definitely be some surprises along the way. But you'll recognize those sexy Irish boys you've all come to love. Watch for them coming soon. (Like many Irish families, sometimes you have to split people up to keep some sort of control.) :)

Happy reading!

Kate Hoffmann

THE MIGHTY QUINNS: RONAN

BY
KATE HOFFMANN

All rights reserved including the right of reproduction in whole or in part in any form. This edition is published by arrangement with Harlequin Books S.A. The text of this publication or any part thereof may not be reproduced or transmitted in any form or by any means, electronic or mechanical, including photocopying, recording, storage in an information retrieval system, or otherwise, without the written permission of the publisher.

This book is sold subject to the condition that it shall not, by way of trade or otherwise, be lent, resold, hired out or otherwise circulated without the prior consent of the publisher in any form of binding or cover other than that in which it is published and without a similar condition including this condition being imposed on the subsequent purchaser.

This is a work of fiction. Names, characters, places, locations and incidents are purely fictional and bear no relationship to any real life individuals, living or dead, or to any actual places, business establishments, locations, events or incidents. Any resemblance is entirely coincidental.

The Mighty Quinns: Ronan © 2014 Peggy A. Hoffmann

ISBN: 978-0-263-90503-8

50-0317

Harlequin (UK) Limited's policy is to use papers that are natural, renewable and recyclable products and made from wood grown in sustainable forests. The logging and manufacturing processes conform to the legal environmental regulations of the country of origin.

Printed and bound in Spain
by Blackprint CPI, Barcelona

First published in Great Britain 2013
by Mills & Boon, an imprint of Harlequin (UK) Limited,
Eton House, 18-24 Paradise Road, Richmond, Surrey TW9 1SR

© Peggy A. Hoffmann 2012

ISBN: 978 0 263 90503 8

30-0213

Harlequin (UK) policy is to use papers that are natural, renewable and recyclable products and made from wood grown in sustainable forests. The logging and manufacturing processes conform to the legal environmental regulations of the country of origin.

Printed and bound in Spain
by Blackprint CPI, Barcelona

Kate Hoffmann has written more than seventy books for Mills & Boon. She spent time as a music teacher, a retail assistant buyer and an advertising exec before she settled into a career as a full-time writer. She continues to pursue her interests in music, theatre and musical theatre, working with local schools in various productions. She lives in south-eastern Wisconsin with her cat, Chloe.

To Brenda, my friend and my editor
and my own best critic.

These Quinns are for you!

Prologue

THE CLOSET WAS dark and quiet. Ronan Quinn clutched the flashlight in his hand, the failing batteries providing a weak shaft of light. Closing his eyes, he tried to banish the disturbing images from his thoughts.

The dreams had started just a few months ago, right after his eighth birthday party. It had been the first party his family had attempted since his parents had disappeared the previous year.

Of course, it hadn't been the same. Birthday parties were what his mother did best. She could turn an ordinary day into the most wonderful, magical event of a person's life. For his seventh birthday, she'd taken him and his whole Cub Scout troop to the aquarium. They'd seen the most amazing thing. There'd been octopus cupcakes with long, licorice tentacles. And games like "Pin The Fin" on the shark. There had even been a fish shaped piñata filled with gum and jawbreakers and all his favorite candy.

At the end of the day, after the party was over and he was exhausted from the excitement, he'd received his gift, a beautiful aquarium, placed on a stand right next to his bed. He remembered how he'd stayed up all night, just watching the fish swimming back and forth in the blue light.

The aquarium was empty now, all the fish dead and the water drained. It was one of those things that had been forgotten once their world had been turned upside down. There was never any time to shop for fish. No one wanted to bother keeping the aquarium clean.

This year, his grandfather and older brothers had planned a party on the family sailboat, gathering ten of Ronan's classmates for a sail on the sound. But when they'd gotten to the dock, Ronan had refused to get on the boat.

Fear had welled up inside of him as he stared at the dark water slapping against the hull. His stomach had begun to roil and his hands had grown ice cold. Ronan knew that if he got on the boat, the sea would swallow him up and pull him down to the very bottom where he would drown.

Dermot had stayed with him on the dock while the rest of the party left. And though his older brother tried to reassure him that everything would be fine, Ronan had seen the looks on his friends' faces. He'd already been marked as being different since his parents' disappearance. Now, he'd be completely alone, the subject of whispers and pity.

Ronan looked down at the book clutched in his arms. The huge picture book of ocean fish had been another gift from his mother. But this one had appeared next to his breakfast one morning. It hadn't been his birthday or Christmas or any type of holiday at all. She'd just decided that he needed the book.

He turned the flashlight onto the pages and stared at the pretty pictures. But when he flipped the page to the chapter on sharks, Ronan slammed the book closed and hugged his knees to his chest.

There were always sharks in his nightmares. Sharks circling in the dark water. He tried not to think about what might have happened to his parents, but the nightmares brought it up again and again.

He'd asked questions that his grandfather and brothers refused to answer. How long could they live in the water? How far could they swim? If they were in the life raft, wouldn't they drift to land? But there were never any explanations. He'd just been told to accept the fact that his mother and father were gone.

But he didn't want to accept it. There was always a chance that they'd be found. Maybe on an island. Or maybe the boat was just floating around in the ocean, the sails torn or lost. Why couldn't anyone see that?

"Ronan?"

His breath caught in his throat and he watched the door, shadows playing with the shaft of light. A few seconds later, the door swung open. His oldest brother, Cameron, stood in front of him.

"What are you doing in here?"

"Nothing," Ronan said.

"You got a book. Are you reading?"

Ronan shook his head.

"Come on," Cameron said. "You need to get back to bed."

"I can't," Ronan said. "I'll have bad dreams again."

Cameron squatted down and rubbed Ronan's knee. "You're having nightmares?"

Ronan nodded. "Bad ones. With sharks. And Mom and Dad are swimming and trying to get away. But the water is dark and they can't see anything." Cameron held out his hands and Ronan crawled into his embrace. "I don't want to go to sleep."

"How about you sleep in my bed tonight," Cameron said.

"Okay," Ronan said, a flood of relief washing over him. Cameron would be able to protect him from the bad dreams. His older brother could do anything.

"You want to bring your book?" Cam asked. He handed it to Ronan. "Your fish book. You really like this book, don't you?"

"Mom gave it to me," Ronan said.

"You like fish? Maybe we could go fishing sometime."

Ronan frowned. He never wanted to go near the ocean again. "I don't like fish that way," he said. "I don't want to go near the black water. It might suck me up and pull me down to the bottom."

"You don't have to be scared of that," Cam said.

But that was one point that Ronan refused to give to his older brother. He was never, ever going to go on the ocean again. "I like my aquarium fish," Ronan ventured.

"You don't have any aquarium fish," Cameron said.

"I know. But I used to like them. They helped me sleep."

"Well, maybe we could ask Grandda if we could go get you some new fish. Would that make you feel better?"

In truth, the only thing that could make Ronan feel better was if his mother was there to tuck him in and his father was there to kiss him goodnight.

Maybe his older brothers could do without that. Cameron was twelve and the twins, Kieran and Dermot were nine, almost ten. Maybe when you got older, hugs and kisses weren't important. But it wasn't a baby thing, was it, to want hugs and kisses?

Ronan reached out and grabbed his brother's hand as they walked out of Ronan's room and into the hall. He needed to be braver. That's what older boys were expected to do. It was time to grow up.

1

THE SUN ROSE as the bus rolled across the state line from New Hampshire into Maine. After four days on the road, crossing the country accompanied by complete strangers, eating at roadside diners and truck stops and sleeping in fits and starts, Ronan was ready to reach his destination.

The sunrise had become an important event for him, something he looked forward to when there was little else to mark the passing time. But now that they'd reached the Atlantic coast, he saw a completely different sunrise, a blaze of color over the blue ocean.

Like Seattle, the passing landscape was dominated by the sea and Ronan felt a hint of familiarity in such a strange, new place. The villages along the route were populated with white clapboard buildings and red brick churches, towering hardwood trees and tidy town squares, and harbors filled with bobbing sailboats.

"Thanks, Grandda," he murmured to himself. He couldn't imagine that his brothers' destinations in New

Mexico, Kentucky and Wisconsin came close to the natural beauty he was seeing here.

The bus ride really hadn't been that bad. As a kid, he'd spent a lot of time alone, riding his bike around the neighborhood or mastering tricks on his skateboard. As he grew older, he'd hiked and climbed and camped, he'd taught himself to ski and snowboard, but always alone, finding comfort in the quiet of a silent mountaintop or a lush forest.

His fondness for solitude had made him a bit of a black sheep in a family of brothers who were impossibly close. Ronan had just never found a proper place for himself. His oldest brother, Cameron, was the responsible one, charged with holding their fractured family together. Dermot was the charmer and Kieran the quiet one. Ronan was the outsider.

It didn't help that Ronan was the only one of the four Quinn boys who harbored an unshakable fear of the water. It had been difficult when every Quinn family activity revolved around boats and sailing. Cam, Dermot and Kieran spent their free time on the water, while Ronan had been forced to find solitary activities on land.

Ronan knew his fear of water had everything to do with what had happened to his parents. He didn't remember many details about that time when the world went black and everyone was sad. Yet, to this day, he remembered the nightmares of cold water and high waves, endless depths and interminable storms, and a deep and utter feeling of loss.

The mother who had comforted him, the father he'd

adored, were suddenly gone, and no one had ever really explained to him how that could have happened. He was the one who held hope the longest, certain that one day, his parents would walk in the door and life would get back to normal.

Ronan didn't mind that he was labeled the odd little brother. It was his place in the family hierarchy and it was comfortable amidst brothers who seemed to thrive on competition. He didn't mind that making friends didn't come easily to him. Or that he was twenty-six and drifted between women the same way he drifted between jobs at the yachtworks.

He didn't want to make plans, he avoided commitment. No one could know what the future held so he didn't think about the future. He lived his days, and his nights, one at a time.

But last week, his grandfather had asked them all to imagine a different life, to put aside the responsibilities they'd taken on as kids and to follow their dreams. To his surprise, the further he got from Seattle and his life there, the more his past began to fade in his mind.

The only dream he'd ever had as a child was more of a fantasy, one where his parents magically reappeared in their lives. Maybe it was time to start making a plan for himself, to focus on a goal and make it come true. Without his family around, he was no longer the black sheep. He was simply Ronan Quinn, a clean slate, a fresh start.

When the bus driver finally called "Sibleyville," Ronan jumped to his feet. He was about to walk into a different life for the next six weeks. A month and a half was what his grandfather had required for this challenge and starting now, Ronan would have to find a job and a place to sleep.

The bus pulled up in front of a drug store and the driver opened the door. "Sibleyville. Anyone for Sibleyville?"

Ronan walked down the aisle, his duffel slung over his shoulder. "Thanks," he said to the driver as he stepped onto the sidewalk.

If there was a picture next to the definition of quaint in the dictionary, this was it, Ronan thought to himself. A neon Rexall Drug sign hung over his head and a variety of merchandise was displayed behind the gleaming plate glass windows on either side of the entrance. The bus pulled away behind him and Ronan turned and watched it disappear down the street.

He drew a deep breath and the salt-tinged sea air filled Ronan's lungs. It was a different smell from home, he mused. Familiar, but different. Small town life was bound to be a change for him. He enjoyed having all the conveniences that a big city provided. But then, people were supposed to be friendlier in places like this. And for a guy who usually depended on himself, Ronan might need the kindness of a few strangers right now.

He walked inside the drug store and immediately noticed the lunch counter along one wall. He still had a little cash left in his pocket so he decided to take a seat and have something to drink while he got his bearings.

An elderly man stepped behind the counter. "What can I get for you?"

"Chocolate malt," he said.

"Made with vanilla ice cream or chocolate?"

The man's New England accent was thick, the words flattened out until Ronan could barely understand. "Vanilla," Ronan said.

He grabbed a menu from the rack in front of him and perused the prices. They served soda fountain treats and sandwiches for lunch, but he'd have to find another spot for breakfast and dinner. "I'm looking for a place to stay," Ronan said. "Something cheap. Can you suggest anything?"

"Well, it's still high season around here, but there are a few boarding houses in town that you could try. Mrs. Morey has a place over on Second Street and Miss Harrington has a few rooms in her house on Whitney. They're pretty fussy about who they rent to. No funny business, if you get my drift."

"Do you know how much they charge?" Ronan asked.

The old man considered the question for a long moment as he prepared the malt. "Can't say that I do."

"I'm also looking for a job," Ronan said.

"There's a board over at the visitors center," he said. "There's always someone looking for help. They'll help you find a room, too, if you ask Maxine. She's usually behind the desk."

He placed the malt in front of Ronan. The old fountain glass was filled to the brim, then topped with whipped cream and a cherry. "That'll be three-ninety-five," he said.

Ronan pulled out his wallet and laid a five on the counter. "Keep the change," he said.

Ronan lingered over the malt, watching as customers came and went, getting a feel for the locals. Everyone in town seemed pretty friendly. There was a certain civility in their manner that he'd never seen in big city residents. Maybe it was because they all knew each other that they went out of their way to greet each other with a friendly hello or a short conversation.

When he finished his malt, Ronan grabbed his duffel and headed out to the visitor's center. The converted railroad station was home to the local merchant's association as well as the tourist office. He went to the job board and scanned the opportunities. There were jobs in restaurants and motels, a job at the local library and one at the marina.

A job at a local oyster farm caught his eye. He glanced around, then pulled the card from the board and tucked it in his pocket. He loved oysters and farming meant that he'd be spending his time outdoors. He couldn't think of a better combination.

Ronan walked over to the hospitality counter and gave the elderly woman sitting behind it a quick smile. "Are you Maxine?"

She nodded. "I am."

"I'm looking for a room. I'm going to be in town for six weeks. It needs to be cheap. I don't have a lot of money."

"We have a couple of boarding houses in town," she said. "And Isiah Crawford rents out a few of his motel rooms on a monthly basis. Let me try Mrs. Morey first."

The woman dialed a number. "Hello, Elvira. It's Maxine down at the Visitor's Center. I have a young man down here looking for a room. Do you have any-thing available?" She paused. "Wonderful. How much?" She scribbled something on her pad, then glanced up at Ronan. "What's your name?"

"Ronan Quinn?"

Maxine's eyes went wide for a moment, then she cleared her throat. "Yes, Elvira, you heard that right. Well, I'm sure he'll understand. If you forgot, you for-got."

Maxine hung up the phone and smiled apologetically. "It seems that she doesn't have a room after all. Some big group coming in."

"Could you try the other boarding house?" he asked.

"I—I don't think Tillie has anything available ei-ther. I just saw her at church this morning and she—she would have mentioned it. Maybe you could try across the river in Newcastle?"

Ronan had the distinct impression that he was getting the runaround. Why were these people suddenly unwill-ing to rent to him? "Maybe you could try the motel?"

With a reluctant smile, she dialed the phone. "Hi there, Josiah. It's Maxine over at the Visitor's Center. I have a young man here named Ronan Quinn and he's looking for a—yes, that's what I said. He's looking for a room. Well, that's a shame. All right. You, too, Josiah."

She hung up the phone again and shrugged. "He doesn't have any vacancies either. Newcastle really is your best option. It's just over the bridge."

"I need to stay here, in Sibleyville," he said. Ronan picked up his duffel bag. "Never mind, I'll find a place on my own."

Maxine forced a smile. "Can I offer you a bit of advice? Don't give them your name. In fact, use a different name entirely. But don't dare tell anyone I gave you this advice. Run along now."

With a soft curse, Ronan walked outside, keeping his temper in check. What the hell was going on here? Did the town have something against the Irish? Or was it just because he was a single guy? From what he could tell, the town thrived on tourism so it didn't make sense they'd turn anyone away. If he'd thought Sibleyville looked like a friendly place at first glance, he'd been sadly mistaken.

He looked down at the card he held. Mistry Bay Oyster Farm. Contact Charlie Sibley. Would a potential employer feel the same? Especially one named after this very village? For now, he'd keep his name to himself until he knew for sure.

"Maybe living a different life is going to be more difficult than I thought it would be," he muttered.

"You NEED TO scrape harder than that," Charlotte Sibley said, running her hand over the rough hull of the skiff. "All this old paint has to come off. If you paint on top of it, it won't stick."

Her fourteen-year-old brother, Garrett, looked up from the task she'd given him and rolled his eyes. "I know what I'm doing."

"Of course you do. You're just not doing a very good job of it. You've been bugging Dad to let you work the boats on your own but you're not willing to put in the effort that comes with it." She ruffled his hair. "Come on, princess, put some muscle into it. We're going to need that skiff this season."

"Who made you the boss of me? You're not the boss of me, Charlie. Dad is."

"And if you haven't noticed, Einstein, Dad is laid up with a bad back. His doctor says he can't work for at least a month or two. He made me the boss of things, so that makes me the boss of you, too."

Garrett muttered something beneath his breath and went back to work. Charlotte smiled to herself. Now that she'd been put in charge of the Mistry Bay oyster farm, it had been a bit of a rocky ascension from worker to boss. Charlie knew the business from top to bottom, after working it for years with her family. And six years away hadn't been long enough to forget the ropes. But being in charge meant that she'd had to rein in the members of the Sibley clan who preferred malingering to hard work.

A knock sounded on the door of the boathouse and Charlotte strode over to the door. She'd been expecting a visit from an up and coming chef from Boston who was visiting the area. Chef Joel Bellingham had already made a name for himself in Boston with one highly rated restaurant and would soon be opening a second— a seafood place that might feature Mistry Bay oysters.

She yanked the door open, but her greeting died in her throat as she came face-to-face with an impossibly handsome man, not much older than she was. He watched her with pale blue eyes, as she tried to regain her breath, his gaze holding hers. Charlie swallowed hard, then cleared her throat. "Hello! Come on in. I hope you didn't have any trouble finding the place." She'd met Bellingham over the phone earlier that morning and had somehow gotten the impression he was much older. This guy could be thirty, tops.

"There was a sign above the door," he said, glancing around.

They stood there for an uncomfortable moment before Charlie could shake herself into action. "How was your trip?" she asked. "The traffic on Highway 1 can be really bad on the weekends."

"It was fine."

He was a man of few words. Charlie felt a stab of disappointment. He obviously wasn't interested in chatting with her. And usually she was so good with customers. But this guy, though stunningly handsome, didn't have much of a personality. "Let me show you around."

The waterfront building served multiple purposes for the family business. Charlie pointed out the shop area where they repaired equipment and boat engines. Housed in the other half of the lower floor was the shipping area, where workers cleaned and sorted oysters before they were boxed to be sent all over the east coast and beyond. As Charlie rattled off her talking points, she realized she wasn't even listening to herself. He stood beside her, nodding politely.

The second floor housed the business offices and a small apartment Charlotte sometimes used when she needed to get away from the craziness at her parents' house. It also included a finely appointed tasting room, modeled after a gourmet kitchen, where they often entertained visitors interested in featuring Mistry Bay oysters at their restaurants or seafood counters. The room overlooked the river and was the perfect setting to talk oysters.

"Mistry Bay is a family business," she said as they walked up the stairs. "We've had the oyster farm for nearly twenty years and we think we have some of the best oysters on the east coast. But I'm a bit prejudiced." She drew a ragged breath. "Why don't we taste some oysters."

He walked beside her into the tasting room and she couldn't help but notice how tall and well built he was, dressed in cargo shorts and a T-shirt that hugged his muscular chest. He hadn't shaved in a few days, but the stubble made him look slightly dangerous. He was like the kind of guy who wore his sex appeal with a casual indifference, as if he didn't care if women noticed him.

Since she'd left Danny in New York over a year ago, Charlotte hadn't found herself attracted to any man. In truth, she'd written off men completely. As long as she was living in Sibleyville, romance was an exercise in futility anyway. But she wasn't averse to indulging in a little fantasy every now and then and Chef Joel Bellingham provided plenty of raw material.

She pointed to a stool at the granite-topped counter then moved to the other side of it to retrieve a bowl of freshly harvested oysters from the refrigerator. As she stood across from him, she laid a folded towel on the counter and grabbed an oyster. Charlotte felt him watching her. She was almost worried to look up, afraid that he'd be able to read her thoughts.

She held the oyster with another towel and popped

the shell open at the hinge. After carefully slicing the meat from the shell, she placed the fresh oyster on a Mistry Bay oyster plate, preserving the liquid in the shell. "Lemon?" she asked.

"No," he said. "I like them plain."

"Can I offer you a pairing? We have champagne, muscadet and ice-cold vodka. All three really enhance the taste of our oysters. Not all together, of course. Each one separately."

"It's eleven in the morning," he said.

"Right."

He regarded her warily. "Champagne would be good. If you're going to join me."

She found a split of bubbly in the fridge, popped it open and poured it into two flutes. Drawing a deep breath, she went into her business pitch as she continued to open oysters. "We ship from September through June and use overnight delivery. That means you can have fresh oysters Tuesday through Saturday mornings. We harvest early in the morning and ship that afternoon."

Charlotte continued to shuck oysters and place them on the plate, describing the attributes of the Mistry Bay oyster in sensual terms. They were plump and juicy, briny and sweet. Usually a half dozen on the half-shell satisfied most customers, but Chef Joel seemed to be particularly hungry.

When she wasn't talking, she was nervously sipping champagne, trying to keep herself from spinning right out of the room. He finally held up his hand at a dozen, then drew a deep breath. "They were really good. Thanks."

Really good? Usually her oysters received more than a "good." Exquisite, delicate, satisfying, better than sex. Really good wasn't that good at all. "Do you have any questions?" she asked.

"Just one. Does this mean I have the job?"

She sent him a quizzical look. "Job? I—I don't understand."

He reached into his pocket and pulled out an index card, then held it out to her. "I found this over at the visitor's center. It said you were looking for help?"

A gasp slipped from her throat. "Wait a second. You're not Chef Joel from Boston?"

"Nope. I'm Ronan. Ronan Smith from Seattle. I don't mind working hard. I'll be here early and stay late. You tell me to do something and it'll be done." He gazed at her silently.

Charlie felt a shiver skitter down her spine and she had to force herself to look away. She cleared her throat. "You ate a dozen oysters," she said. "Did you think that was part of the interview?"

"I just thought you were showing me the product. And I was hungry."

She really couldn't blame him for the mix-up. She'd been caught off guard from the moment she set eyes on him. The fluttery feeling in her stomach and the buzzing in her head had made it impossible to think clearly. Maybe if she'd had her wits about her, she might have seen his confusion sooner.

"So, do I have the job?" he asked again.

"Come with me," Charlotte said. She had just posted the job yesterday. Considering the other employment opportunities available, she hadn't expected such a quick response. Nor such an interesting prospect. But here was guy who set her heart racing and she had a perfectly good reason to keep him around a little longer.

"The job is hard, with long hours. The pay isn't great, but with the hours you work, you should make a decent living. Are you going to have a problem with that?"

"Nope," he said as he followed her downstairs.

She led him over to the inverted skiff. "This is my brother, Garrett. Garrett, this is Ronan Smith. He's interviewing for the job. Give him your scraper."

"No problem," Garrett said, handing Ronan the paint scraper. "I'm going home, Charlie."

Charlotte didn't argue this time. She was glad to be rid of her little brother. She certainly didn't need him watching her fall all over herself around the gorgeous new employee. "Cut the lawn when you get home. You know Dad can't do it and Mom is too busy."

"Yeah, yeah," Garrett said.

"Teenagers," she murmured as they watched Garrett walk out the door. When she turned back to Ronan, she caught him staring, his blue eyes direct and intense.

"You're Charlie?" he asked. "You're the boss?"

"Yes. Charlotte. Charlie. Sibley."

"I was expecting a man."

"And I was expecting a chef," she countered.

"What do you want me to call you?"

She caught a look in his eyes that appeared to be amusement. Was he just toying with her? Or had she completely lost control of this interview. "You don't have the job yet." She picked up the paint scraper and safety glasses and handed them to him. "If you want the job, show me what you can do with this scraper first."

He nodded. And for the first time since they met, he smiled. To Charlie, it was as if the morning mist had suddenly parted and the sunshine shone down. He was even more attractive, if that was possible.

Men who looked like Ronan Smith usually learned to wield their charm early on. By the time they reached their teens, they knew the effect they had on the opposite sex and used it to their advantage. But Ronan seemed reluctant to use his God-given advantages.

He set to work on the skiff, a shower of paint chips flying off with each stroke. Charlie watched him for a moment, her gaze falling on the finely cut muscles in his arms. A shiver skittered down her spine and she turned and hurried back upstairs to clean up the tasting room. A bit of privacy gave her a chance to take a deep breath and focus her runaway thoughts—on Ronan Smith. It was an odd name, Ronan.

She grabbed the bottle and guzzled the remainder of the champagne, then opened another split. He'd mentioned he was from Seattle. She really ought to ask for references. Or a resume. For all she knew, he could be a criminal or a con artist—or a competitor, out to get an inside look at their operation.

Sliding onto one of the stools, she opened up another oyster and slurped it down. Ronan was a complete enigma. But then, when it came to men, she really didn't know what she was doing. She'd only had one romantic relationship in her life and that had lasted six years.

She and Danny had started dating when they were

juniors in high school, playing opposite each other in the school musical. When they graduated, they were both determined to chase their dreams on Broadway.

But New York was a rude awakening. Danny was easily discouraged and took a full time job selling cell phones. After some minor parts in a criminal drama, a series of commercials for generic laundry detergent, and an appearance in an off-off-Broadway play, Charlie was beginning to break through.

But as she got more work, Danny became more and more distant—and jealous. Their relationship began to fracture and Charlie realized that New York wasn't where she wanted to be. So, she moved out and came home to Sibleyville, older and a little wiser.

She glanced up at the chef's mirror above the granite counter. A groan slipped from her throat. Her chestnut hair looked liked a tangle of seaweed. Charlie grabbed a clean oyster brush from the drawer next to the fridge and ran it though the shoulder-length strands, then pinched her cheeks to give herself some color.

She rarely wore make-up when she was working and usually didn't care to dress in anything that showed off her figure. Yet she couldn't help but regret that it wasn't the New York City actress Charlotte Sibley that opened the door to Ronan Smith rather than the oyster farmer Charlie Sibley.

She looked at herself in the mirror once more. Though she could pretend to be a myriad of interesting and exotic characters, Charlie knew that the woman she was would have to be enough.

Shaking her head, she walked to the door, but found

herself off balance from the champagne she'd guzzled. If she was going to hire Ronan, than she'd have to keep her feelings to herself and her wits about her. A man like Ronan probably had women drooling over him everyday. And Charlie had never aspired to be one of the crowd.

RONAN SMOOTHED HIS hand over the hull of the twenty-foot skiff. The boat was old, maybe sixty or seventy years old from the clues he'd found in the construction. Nowadays, most commercial outfits chose fiberglass boats for their easy upkeep and long life.

"How's it going?"

He glanced up to see Charlie watching him. Jaysus, she was pretty. Her wavy dark hair framed a beautiful face, each of her features a perfect complement to the others. She had the kind of beauty that made him want to sit her down in front of him so he might study her in greater detail, like a fine painting or a famous sculpture.

"Good. This is a beautiful boat," he said. "I love the lines."

"It's old," she said.

"They don't make them like this anymore. I think the best boats are made of wood."

"My dad would totally agree with you." Charlie came closer to examine his work. "You're very thorough," she murmured.

The compliment pleased him, more so because it came from her. "This scraper is kind of dull. If you've got a way for me to sharpen it, I'd get more done. And you might want to use a better grade of marine paint next time," he said. "If you apply it properly and maintain it, you shouldn't have to repaint as often." He stopped himself. Now he was sounding like the boss.

"You know something about boats?" she asked, raising an eyebrow.

"Yeah," Ronan said. "Just a little."

"You said you were from Seattle. What are you doing in Maine?"

"Just traveling," Ronan said. "Seeing America."

"Well, if you're willing to work hard, I'll pay you a fair wage," she said. "We have the office and shop here in town. And our nursery and hatchery is out at Kepley Pond. Then we grow out the oysters at Mistry Bay."

Kepley Pond. Mistry Bay. That sounded like a lot of water. Since he'd been eight years old, Ronan made a point to stay off the water, at least the ocean. But he wanted this job and he'd need to put his fears aside. Maybe it was time to face the past. Besides, no one ever got lost at pond or at bay like they got lost at sea.

"You've done good work on the boat," she said. "The job is yours, if you'd like it."

"There is one thing," he said. "I need to find somewhere to stay. I was hoping you might be able to help me."

"We've got a small apartment upstairs next to the office. I could rent that to you," she said. "As long as you're quiet and tidy, I don't see any problems."

"Great," he said. Ronan knew he ought to tell her his real name. She didn't seem like the type to discriminate, although he still hadn't figured out what the problem was with the rest of the town. "I tried to find a place in town, but no one wanted to rent to me."

"Why not?"

He shrugged. "I don't know. As soon as I told them my name, they suddenly didn't have a room to rent."

"Ronan?" she asked. "Or Smith?"

"Quinn," he said. "My name is Ronan Quinn, not Smith." He paused and watched as surprise came over her pretty features. "See. That's the look right there. So it is the name."

She laughed softly and then a sudden hiccup stopped her. Pressing her fingers to her lips, she sent him an apologetic smile. "Yeah. People around here have a pretty big grudge against anyone named Quinn."

"How could they have a grudge against me? They don't even know me."

Charlotte shrugged. "Well, I don't really believe in all the silliness. Spells and curses and witches. I'm willing to give you a job, Ronan Quinn. And a place to stay, if you want."

"What did this Quinn do to make everyone mad?"

"It's a complicated story," Charlie said, waving him off.

"Don't you think I ought to hear it, so I know what I'm up against?"

She shook her head. "If I tell you the story, you'll think we're all so crazy that you'll want to leave town. And I need an oysterman." She pointed to his duffel. "Grab your bag and I'll show you the apartment."

Ronan breathed a silent sigh of relief. "I didn't mean

to lie about my name. I was just trying to figure things out."

"No matter," she said, walking him back upstairs.

When they got to the second floor, a doorway opened into a lobby for a spacious office opposite the tasting room. "Things usually get busy in here in the afternoon when we're preparing packing lists and labels for our shipments but all that starts next week."

She showed him a comfortable one-bedroom apartment with a galley kitchen and a comfortable bed. A bay window overlooked the water and he could hear the metallic clank of the boat riggings through the glass. "This is nice," he said.

"If you need an advance to buy groceries, I can help you out there."

"I could use that," he said. "And I can finish the skiff today. I'll work on it all night if I have to."

"Great," she murmured. Charlie stood in front of him, her gaze flitting nervously around the room. Though Ronan had tried to hide his attraction to his new boss, he hadn't really considered that she might be attracted to him. As she shifted nervously, her fingers twisted together, he decided to test a theory.

He leaned a bit closer, just a few inches, waiting for her response. Would she lean in as well, and close her eyes, expecting a kiss?

"Bathroom," she said, turning away.

He followed her into the tiny bathroom. It looked like the room had once been a small closet and they had to struggle to move around. When they finally maneuvered themselves into a comfortable position, they were so close Ronan could feel the heat from her body.

"You—you have to jiggle the handle on the toilet to get it to stop running. And the—the tub drains real slow," she said, glancing over her shoulder. "So it's probably best to use the shower stall instead. Unless you're a bath guy." She paused. "Most guys aren't."

He leaned a bit closer and when she turned back to him, she sucked in a sharp breath, startled by the move. Charlie retreated a step, but didn't realize how close she was to the edge of the tub. She began to lose her balance, flailing her arms.

Ronan had to think quick and decided to save her the pain and humiliation of falling into the bathtub. He slipped his arm around her waist and pulled her against his body. But this didn't have the intended effect at all. She shifted to evade slamming up against his chest and ran face first into the edge of the door.

"Ow!" she cried, covering her eye with her palm.

"Are you all right?" Ronan asked.

Charlie pulled her hand away and shook her head. "I think I'm bleeding." She struggled to get to the medicine chest above the sink and Ronan wrapped his hands around her waist.

"Out. I'll get them." Ronan found a box of band-aids and then grabbed a washcloth from the towel rack and soaked it with cold water. He found Charlie leaning against the kitchen counter, her fingers doing little to staunch the flow of blood.

"Let me look," Ronan said.

Wincing, she pulled her hand away. "It's bleeding a lot. Does it look like it needs stitches?"

Ronan dabbed at the small cut. "No. It's tiny. There's a lot of blood. Here, hold this."

She pressed the cold cloth to her head as he fumbled to open the bandage. "Sorry," she murmured.

"What are you apologizing for? It's not your fault." Ronan wanted to reach out and touch her cheek, to see if it was as soft as it looked. His gaze drifted down to her mouth. If they were going to spend time together, it was going to be hard to resist kissing her.

Though Ronan didn't work hard at romance, he had enjoyed the regular company of a number of beautiful women. But he usually liked to spend his free time in solitary pursuits, which left little for long-term, serious relationships. Still, he was curious about this particular woman. What was it about Charlie Sibley that he found so intriguing?

"Hello! Anyone home?"

She forced a smile. "That would be the real Joel Bellingham," Charlie murmured.

Ronan drew her wash cloth away and then neatly covered the cut with a small band-aid. "There. All better."

"Thanks," she said.

"No problem."

She stared at him for a long moment and Ronan's gaze fell to her lips, so lush and slightly parted. He wanted to lean forward and take just a quick taste, but she seemed to sense what was on his mind and quickly stepped back.

He watched as she hurried out of the apartment, her footsteps fading on the stairs. They'd have plenty of time to figure this all out, Ronan mused. A lot could happen in six weeks.

2

CHARLIE WALKED CHEF Joel to the door, then shook his hand. "We'll be looking forward to your first order. Please, don't hesitate to call me if you have any questions or concerns."

He patted the folder she'd given him. "I've got everything I need right here," he said. "It was a pleasure to meet you, Charlotte. We'll talk soon."

She closed the door behind him and smiled. Mistry Bay oysters in one of the best new restaurants in Boston would be a huge account for the farm.

The effects of the champagne had worn off and she counted herself lucky that she'd been able to complete her sale pitch without an embarrassing incident. What had she been thinking? Ronan Quinn had thrown her into a complete tizzy.

"A tizzy," she murmured to herself. It was the perfect word for how she felt when she thought about Ronan. In fact, the word applied to her everyday life lately.

Since she'd been back from New York, she'd been waiting for some sign, some new direction for her life.

Charlie had always had a laser-like focus on a goal. At first, it had been the move after high school, and then auditioning and attending acting classes and finding an agent. After that came the jobs, each one bigger and better than the last.

But here in Sibleyville, there was no goal anymore, besides getting up in the morning and going to sleep at night. She was drifting aimlessly through life and she couldn't seem to stop herself. It really was time to make a few hard decisions about what she really wanted to do. Cursing softly, she climbed the stairs to the second floor.

When she got to the tasting room, she quickly tidied up the mess from Chef Joel's visit. She'd heard the shower through the door of the apartment, but the water was off now. Drawing a deep breath, she crossed to the door and rapped on it softly.

The door swung open and Ronan stood on the other side, shirtless, his cargo shorts riding low on his hips. His hair was damp and droplets clung to the smooth expanse of his chest.

Charlie drew a deep breath and the scent of soap and shampoo filled her head. Her fingers twitched and she fought the urge to reach out and smooth the water from his skin. "I thought it might be good to show you the nursery and the farm," she said. "You're going to be working at both."

"All right," Ronan said. "Just let me grab a shirt."

She swallowed hard. "I'll just wait outside in the truck."

The image of Ronan Quinn half-naked was now

burned into her brain and it was a memory she didn't really want to forget. His body was beautiful, lean yet muscular, every limb in perfect proportion. It had taken every last ounce of her resolve to walk away.

She could have reached out and touched him, knowing that he might take the action as an invitation. But what then? Would he have kissed her? She wanted to believe that she saw desire in his eyes, but she'd only ever been with one man and that gave her little to use as a reference.

The only option left to her was to wait until he made the first move. At least then she wouldn't be humiliated by misreading his signals. Charlie hurried down the stairs, stumbling on the last step and grabbing the rail for balance. But maintaining her composure was going to be the difficult part. Whenever she looked at him, her knees got wobbly and her brain refused to function.

Charlie grabbed a brochure from the rack near the front door, then walked outside to her SUV. She hopped behind the wheel, the started it up, a love song blaring from the radio. With a soft curse, she reached out and turned it off. The last thing she needed was to start thinking about romance. Besides, if the curse was to be believed, then falling in love within the village limits of Sibleyville was impossible.

A few minutes later, Ronan stepped outside, squinting his eyes against the noonday sun. He slipped his sunglasses on. She honked the horn and Ronan started toward her. When he was settled in the passenger seat, she handed him the brochure. "There's a map inside. You'll need to learn how to get to the pond and the bay by road as well as by water. I'll show you by water to-morrow, but today, we'll go by land."

"I don't have a car," he said.

"How did you get here?" she asked as she pulled out of the parking lot onto the street.

"Bus?"

Charlie frowned. Why would a guy like Ronan be traveling by bus? He might as well have told her that he'd rode up on a camel. "Bus?"

"Yeah. It was part of the deal," he said.

"What kind of deal was that?" A sudden sting of doubt pricked at her thoughts. "You didn't just get out of prison, did you?"

This time he laughed, a deep, resonant sound that caused her heart to flutter. She glanced over at him and took in his smile. God, he was really handsome when he smiled. "Did you?"

"No," he said. "My grandfather sent me on this trip. He picked the place, bought me the bus ticket and sent me on my way."

"Why?"

He paused for a long moment, as if he was decid-ing exactly how much to reveal to her. "When me and my three brothers were just kids, our folks died in an accident."

"I'm sorry to hear that," Charlie murmured.

"We all worked together on the family business," he said. "We build custom sailing yachts. Quinn Yachtworks in Seattle."

"So that's why you knew so much about the skiff." She risked another glance over at him and caught him staring at her from behind his dark glasses. "Why would he send you away?"

"He wanted us all to live a different life for a while. To figure out if we wanted to continue on with the family business or strike out on our own."

"So you decided to try oyster farming," she said. "I'm not sure that was a very sensible choice. It's not nearly as glamorous as building yachts. It's a lot of dirty, sweaty work. And some days, the mosquitoes are so thick they'll carry you away."

"I don't mind working hard," he said. "And I like being outside."

"All right," she said. "Now, watch that map because this next turn is kind of tricky. It's easy to miss."

Charlie pointed out the sign for the hatchery right before she turned down the narrow, winding road to Kepley Pond. "My dad's brother, Uncle Jake, runs the hatchery and nursery."

She stopped the SUV in front of the hatchery building, then jumped out and waited for Ronan to join her. "This is where we start," she said. "Kepley Pond. It's really not a pond, but an estuary. We bring adult stock into the nursery from the bay. Usually, oysters spawn in mid-summer, when the water reaches a certain temperature, but we gradually bring the temperature up, forcing them to lay their eggs in the spring. We also grow phytoplankton here to feed the larvae. When they're ready, we move the seed oysters into an upweller system beneath those six docks. We also sell seed oysters to other farmers in the area."

Charlie led him down to the pond. Long wooden

docks jutted out into the brackish water. "As they grow, we put them in containers that sit on the bottom of the pond, giving them space so that they grow evenly. And when they're big enough, we plant them out in the bay."

"How do you do that?"

"We toss them overboard with a snow shovel. Very high tech. Maine oysters grow slower in the colder water so they'll stay in the bay for about three or four years before we harvest them. We do that a lot of different ways, mostly dredging. In some areas we culture them in lantern nets. A few times a year at low tide, we can harvest them by hand." She smiled. "So, that's oyster farming in a...an oyster shell."

They walked to the end of one of the docks and Charlie showed him the upwell system. When she'd replaced the cover, she watched as he sat down at the end of the dock, as if his thoughts were elsewhere.

She sat down beside him, glancing over to study his expression. "Is there something wrong?"

He shook his head, his gaze still fixed on a point on the pond. "So, I'm going to have to go out on the water with a boat?"

"Yeah. That's how we plant and harvest. Can't you swim?"

"Oh, yeah, I can swim. I'm just not a real big fan of boats. And deep...dark water."

"That's going to be a problem," she said. Why would he have come to an oyster farm for work if he didn't like the water? Oysters didn't grow in a cornfield.

"No, it won't," he said, his voice on edge. "I need the job. I'm just going to have to suck it up and do it."

"We wear life vests," she said. "If you fall overboard, we'll pull you out. My brothers and sisters fall in all the time." She paused. "Why are you afraid of the water?"

"It's just something from my childhood. It really doesn't make a lot of sense."

"You can tell me," Charlie said.

"My parents—they were lost at sea," he said, turned to her. "They were sailing a yacht across the Pacific and it disappeared. Probably sank during a storm. Or maybe it got hit by a cargo ship. Nobody knows."

"Oh, my God," Charlie said. "That must have been horrible."

"After that, I couldn't bring myself to get onboard a boat and whenever I tried I'd get kind of freaked out."

Charlie reached out and took his hand, covering it with hers. "I guess we could work on that," she said.

"You don't have to pay me until I can do the work," he said. "It's my problem. I'll work it out."

"Sure. Why don't we take a little boat ride tonight," she said. "A test ride, and see how you feel. These estuaries are a lot different than the open ocean."

He stared down at their hands, then wove his fingers through hers. When he looked back up, their gazes met for a long moment. Ronan leaned closer and in a heartbeat, his lips met hers in a soft, lingering kiss. He drew back, then decided it wasn't enough, cupping her face in his hands and deepening the kiss.

It was so unexpected, but not at all unwanted. Charlie was afraid to breathe, afraid to make a sound for fear that the spell that had fallen over them would suddenly burst. It had been so long since a man had touched her this way, but all the old familiar feelings came back in a rush.

When he finally pulled back, a long sigh slipped from his body. He pressed his forehead to hers, still holding her face in his hands. "Was that all right?" he murmured.

Charlie wasn't sure if he wanted permission or if he was asking for a review of his technique. "It was very all right," she said. "I—I mean, good. Very good. And all right, too."

He smiled. "So I can do it again?"

"Sure," she said. "Right now?"

"Later," he said. Ronan pushed to his feet, then held out his hand. When she stood beside him, he drew her hand to his mouth and pressed his lips to her wrist. "What's next, boss?"

In truth, Charlie would have been happy to continue what they were doing. But maybe later would be better. "I think I'm going to take you home to meet the folks," she said.

He gasped. "What?"

"You kissed me. You know what that means. My mama and daddy are going to want to look you over."

"You're kidding, right?"

She laughed. "Yeah. But my dad will want to meet you. He has to meet everyone we hire. He's the president of the company."

"All right."

"I won't tell him about your fear of boats. I think I'll keep that to myself a little bit longer," she promised.

"GARRETT SIBLEY, CLOSE that door! You're letting flies in!"

Charlie's brother ran down the front steps of the porch, then turned back to grin at Ronan. "It's Indian food tonight," he said. "If I were you, I'd turn around and get out of here before she forces you to eat it."

Ronan turned to Charlie and she gave him a reassuring smile. "My mother likes to try cooking new cuisines. Don't worry, if it's really bad, we'll get something else to eat later. Just tell her it's good and eat really slowly."

"I like Indian food," he said.

"Me, too. But this won't taste like any Indian food you've ever had. Last month, she was mastering German food and everything tasted like vinegar."

The Sibley family lived in a sprawling white clapboard Victorian, set on a beautiful tree-lined street in the heart of Sibleyville. It was the biggest house in town by far, a testament to the family's position in a town that bore their name.

They climbed the steps to the wide porch, lined with old wicker furniture and decorated with hanging baskets of colorful flowers. Ronan heard another shout from inside the house and a moment later, a young girl came running out the door. "Garrett, come back here. You have to help me finish folding the laundry." She froze when she saw Charlie and Ronan, sending Ronan a suspicious look.

"This is my sister, Libby," Charlie said. "She's thirteen. Libby, this is Ronan. He's going to be working for us."

She rolled her eyes and continued her call for her brother, running down the steps and shouting his name.

"Is your whole family going to be here?"

She nodded. "Isaac is a senior in college and Abby is a sophomore. They're in college but they still live at home. Jane is eighteen and Ethan is sixteen and both are in high school. Don't try to remember them all."

"I'm not sure I could," Ronan said.

"When they're all around, things can get kind of crazy, but once you get used to them, they'll seem almost normal. Whatever you do, don't look the dog directly in the eyes and if my brother Ethan asks you to pull his finger, don't do it."

"If this is going to be a problem, I can always pick up some dinner at the grocery store," Ronan said.

"No, no, my dad is going to want to meet you before you start work. He has to approve my choices."

"Your dad hurt his back?"

"Last season. He was moving a crate of oysters off the boat and onto the dock. He just twisted the wrong way and herniated a disc." She reached for the door. "Ready?"

"I guess so."

How bad could it be, Ronan wondered. Charlie was nice enough. Actually, she was more than that. She was funny and sexy and smart. But there was something else about her he found attractive, a warmth that he rarely saw in the women he'd dated.

She pulled the door open and he stepped inside. The old Victorian was decorated in a style that Ronan could describe as early twenty-first century chaos mixed with beautiful antiques. The furniture was tattered but comfortable. Every available space was filled with some bizarre knickknack or strange painting. On one shelf alone, Ronan saw a stuffed raccoon, an old microscope, a doll with one eye, and a paint-by-numbers portrait of FDR.

"Look what the cat dragged in!" A young man walked through the room, giving Ronan the once over. He resembled Charlotte with her bronze eyes and wavy dark hair. "If I were you, I'd leave right now. It's Indian food."

"Isaac, this is Ronan Quinn."

Isaac's eyebrow shot up. "You brought a Quinn home? Maybe I will stay for dinner." He turned around. "Hey, Abs, come and see what Charlie brought home."

In less than a minute, Ronan realized that he probably should have opted for dinner alone. He could feel the energy in the house, as if the walls were vibrating and the roof was about the blow off.

An older woman appeared in the dining room, her graying hair twisted into a haphazard knot on top of her head. She held a fly swatter in her hand. "Hello, dear. You brought a friend. I'm cooking Indian tonight. Chicken tandoori. I was supposed to marinate the chicken in yogurt, but I had to use cottage cheese instead. And Delbert didn't have anything called garam masala down at the grocery, so I had to leave that out. You don't know what that is, do you?"

"Mama, this is Ronan Quinn. He's going to be helping us out for a few weeks."

She blinked in surprise. "Quinn? Really. Well, now,

that's very interesting. We'll have something good to talk about over dinner. I suppose you haven't had a very enthusiastic welcome in town. But our family really doesn't set much store in that curse. Charlotte, offer the man a drink."

"Curse?" Ronan asked.

"Is this the Quinn?" A young woman, about nineteen or twenty came running into the room. "I'm Abigail. Gosh, I almost expected you to have horns and a forked tail. You're totally hot." She turned to Charlie. "Good move, sissy."

"Charlie, if that's you, I need you in here right away."

"That's my dad," she said. She grabbed Ronan's hand and pulled him along through the spacious living room. "Come on. Let's introduce you to the big guy. Then I'll get you that drink."

When Charlie had called her father the "big guy", she'd used an apt description. The man sitting behind the desk in the library was tall and broad-shouldered. He struggled to his feet and held out his hand. "Peyton Sibley," he said.

"Daddy, this is Ronan Quinn. He answered the ad I put up at the visitor's center. He's from Seattle and he knows a lot about boats."

"Well, Charlotte, that was a lovely introduction," Peyton said as he sat down again, "but maybe we should let this young man speak for himself. You say your name is Quinn?"

Ronan nodded.

"I suppose you haven't had a very enthusiastic reception here in Sibleyville."

"Nobody has really explained that to me, sir. Maybe you could."

"No, no, no. We don't really believe in all that silliness. So, you think you can help us out here?"

"Yes, sir."

"You just listen to Charlotte. She'll teach you the ropes. If you get stuck working with my brother, Jake, do not let him goad you into talking about religion, politics or his three ex-wives. And if you're staying for dinner, please tell my wife that whatever she's been cooking all day—"

"Tandoori chicken," Charlie said.

"I have no idea what that is, but I'm sure I'll regret it in another four to six hours." He opened the drawer of his desk and pulled out a big bottle of antacid tablets. Peyton popped a few into his mouth and offered the bottle to Ronan. "Might want to get a jump on it."

"No, that's fine, sir. I have a pretty strong stomach."

He slammed his hand on the surface of his desk. "Charlotte, I approve! Put this man on the payroll. Anyone who calls me 'sir' can't be all bad. Even if he is named Quinn."

"Thanks, Daddy," Charlotte said. She grabbed Ronan's arm and pulled him along, back out into the foyer. "See, that wasn't so bad."

"For a Quinn," Ronan muttered.

"Why don't you go sit out on the porch and I'll get us something to drink," she said.

Ronan nodded and headed back outside. He walked to the end of the porch and sat down on a swing. As he pushed off with his toes, he felt the movement relax him. This entire day had been just a little strange. And the longer it lasted, the stranger it became. Except for one thing—that kiss he'd shared with Charlie.

He drew a deep breath. That had been the only thing that made perfect sense to him. And he didn't want to wait to do it again.

"I hope beer is all right," Charlie said as she walked out the front door. She glanced around, then saw him on the end of the porch and slowly approached. She handed him the bottle, then leaned up against the railing and watched him. "Are you all right?"

"Maybe you ought to tell me why everyone in Sibleyville has a problem with me. I think I need to know a little more about this curse."

She sat down beside him, her shoulder brushing against his. It was an innocent contact, but it sent his senses spinning. He could feel her warmth, smell her hair, listen to the soft sound of her voice. She excited him and relaxed him all at once. How was that possible?

"It's really kind of silly. And it's not you. Just your last name." She paused as if to gather her thoughts. "Her name was Bridget Quinn, but everyone called her Bridie. She lived in Sibleyville about a hundred and fifty years ago and worked as a maid in my great-great-great grandfather's home. She came from Ireland with her daughter to escape the potato famine. Her daughter, Moira, fell in love with Edward Sibley, my great-great-grandfather and they wanted to get married, but his father refused permission. When Edward wouldn't give up Moira, his father started a rumor that Bridie was a witch and the folks in Sibleyville ran her and her daughter out of town. But before she left, Bridie cursed the town."

"Good for her," Ronan said. "What was the curse?"

"That no one would ever find love within the village limits of Sibleyville. And no one ever has."

Ronan frowned. "The curse worked?"

"In one hundred and fifty years, no man and woman from Sibleyville have ever married each other. To find love, we have to go out of town. We even have a match-maker who helps out with that."

"But Sibleyville is pretty small. That isn't unusual."

"For one-hundred and fifty years?" She shrugged. "There was one couple and every one thought the curse would be broken, but it didn't work out."

"Who was that?"

"Just a couple of infatuated kids." She turned and gave him a smile. "You want to see something really cool?"

"Sure," Ronan said.

They walked around the house to the backyard, a large expanse of grass surrounded by deep gardens and a white picket fence. A huge oak tree stood at the rear of the lot and Charlie led him over to it and pointed up.

Hidden amidst the leafy boughs was an intricate tree house with all the gingerbread detail of the main house. "Oh, man. Look at that. I always wanted a tree house when I was a kid."

"Pull on the rope and a ladder will drop down."

Ronan did as she told him and climbed the ladder. When he was halfway up, he turned to look down on her. "Are you coming up?"

"Right after you," she said.

He had to open a trap door to get inside, but once he was standing, he was amazed at the amount of room in the little house. Charlie joined him, then closed the trap door.

Hinged wood panels covered the top part of the walls and Charlie pulled each panel up and hooked it overhead, allowing the breeze to blow through the tree house. Ronan stood at one of the windows and looked down into the yard. "I can barely remember my childhood," he said. "I know I should be able to, but all of it was so…dark."

Charlie stood next to him, leaning in until her shoulder rubbed against his. "You can't remember one happy time?"

"No." He stared down at her, transfixed by the strange color of her eyes. "We didn't have the freedom most kids have. You know, what I'm talking about. The time to be completely carefree, without any responsibilities. From the time my parents disappeared, we all had a job to do. We had to work hard and help my grandfather because he was good enough to take us in." Ronan had never really opened up about his childhood, but now, he couldn't seem to stop talking.

"Was there any doubt that he would?"

Ronan shrugged. "Probably not. But when you're an orphan, you're always living on the edge of disaster. At least, that's what we thought. We just never laughed. It was almost as if having fun would have been disrespectful to the memory of my parents. Even though I know they would have wanted us to be happy." He glanced over at her, and shook his head. "I've never talked about this before. Not to anyone."

"I'm a good listener," Charlie said.

"You are." He smiled and she turned to him. And instant later, she wrapped her arms around his neck and kissed him. Her lips parted and she let the kiss play out, their tongues teasing and tasting. And when she was finished, she stepped back.

"Please tell me that's part of the job."

"If it was, we probably wouldn't get much else done," Charlie said. "I just thought it was important that we got that out of the way."

He chuckled softly. "You've been thinking about it?"

"No," she said. "I mean, yes, I was. It just seemed to be hanging between us, so I thought I'd get it out there so we wouldn't have to keep wondering."

"I'm not sure that worked," Ronan said. "Because now I can't stop thinking about it."

RONAN STOOD ON the pier, staring down into the skiff. Charlie held out her hand, sending him an encouraging smile. "We're not going anywhere. You're just going to step into the skiff and sit for a while. I promise, we won't untie the lines from the dock. Come on. Baby steps."

After a rollicking dinner with her family, Charlie was grateful for the relative peace and quiet of the waterfront. Gulls circled above and every now and then, the strains of a rock song drifted out the door of a nearby pub. It was a perfect summer night, a cool breeze blowing off the ocean, the water calm. And now that she was alone with Ronan, all she could think about was kissing him again.

Her mind wandered back to their encounter in the tree house. Charlie had never been a patient person. When there was something to be done, she just got it done. Apparently, that now applied to men. She'd felt the attraction between them, knew what he was thinking about and couldn't help herself.

Thankfully, Ronan didn't seem to mind a more aggressive approach. It was obvious that he enjoyed the kiss. But this next time, she was going to let him take the lead. She didn't want to seem like some love-starved fool—even though that's exactly what she felt like.

"You said you swim. What's different about that water?" Charlie asked.

"It has sides," he said. "The pool has sides. And a bottom. And no sharks or killer whales."

"All right," she said. "This river has sides. We're on one side and you can see the other right over there," she said, pointing toward Newcastle. "And I can assure you, it has a bottom. About twenty feet down in the center. Does that make you feel better?" She wiggled her fingers. "Baby steps."

Taking a deep breath, Ronan stepped off the dock into the skiff. "There you go," she said, reaching out to give his hands a squeeze. "See, that wasn't so bad. How do you feel?"

"Good," Ronan murmured. He quickly stepped out of th skiff and back onto the dock. "Surprisingly good." He rubbed his hands on the front of his shorts. "I'm really not feeling bad at all."

"All right. I'm going to let you decide what we do next. When you're ready." She sat down in the seat behind the controls and waited.

He stepped down into the boat again. "I don't feel so bad."

"You could sit here next to me. See how that feels."

He did as he was told, his fingers clutching onto the back of the seat.

Charlie leaned toward him. "You could kiss me again," she suggested.

"I think that might just confuse my issues."

"Maybe that's exactly what you need."

He grinned and shook his head. "Why don't you start the engine?"

Charlie sat behind the wheel and turned the key. An instant later, the outboard rumbled. She watched Ronan, but nothing in his expression changed. "We could just take a little ride across the river. That might be a good start."

He nodded, fixing his gaze across the river at the destination. "All right. Let's go. Just do it before I can say no."

She tossed off the lines, then lowered the engine into the water and pushed the throttle into reverse. The skiff was easy to maneuver, low in the water and wide enough to offer a stable ride. Charlie kept a close eye on Ronan, but he seemed remarkably calm.

"Are you all right?"

"No," he said. "Do I look all right?"

"You look good. I—I mean, you look calm."

"I don't feel calm. I feel like I'm ready to jump out of my skin." He drew a ragged breath. "Go faster."

"Not around here," she said. "No wake. But if we go further down the river we can."

He nodded. "All right, let's go." Charlie turned the boat down the river. Like most of the waterways on the seacoast of Maine, it was really more of a narrow point in an estuary. The water in Sibleyville was brackish and still affected by the tides.

Charlie smiled against the cool evening air as it blew through her hair. She couldn't think of a more perfect end to the day. There was every chance that Ronan would kiss her again and maybe, after that, something more intimate might happen.

She couldn't deny that she'd considered the possibility. She was a young, healthy woman, with normal sexual desires. It was easy to forget those desires when there was no possibility of satisfying them. But this man had suddenly dropped into her life. It was only natural to take advantage, right?

The river widened significantly south of Sibleyville, pushing the shores out into the distance. She slowed the boat, wondering at Ronan's reaction. "We can turn back if you like."

Ronan shook his head. "No, not yet."

"Battle Cove is right over there," she said. She brought the skiff around and headed toward the entrance to the cove. It was a pretty little spot that she used to come to with her siblings when they wanted to swim in the summer.

Stone cliffs surrounded the shallow water, the cliffs

lined with tall pines. She dropped the anchor in the middle of the cove and turned off the engine. It was so quiet, they could hear the birds singing on shore.

"This is better," he said. "It's like a swimming pool."

"It is." She shifted in her seat to face him. "I think you're doing pretty well."

"I want to puke."

"Don't do that," she said.

"I'm fine." He ran his fingers through his hair. "Although who knows what kind of nightmares this is going to bring tonight."

"You haven't tried going out on a boat since you were a kid?"

"There wasn't a reason. I didn't need to be on the water. Man, that fear was so huge in my mind." He met her gaze. "Maybe it would be different out on the ocean. Just the thought of that makes me a little queasy."

"Well, we stick pretty close to shore," she said. "And the bay is much wider where we harvest, but it's not deep. I think you'll be all right."

He reached out and took her hand. "I've had a pretty unusual day. When my grandfather sent me here, I didn't expect this."

"What?"

"You," he said.

Her breath caught in her throat and Charlie had to remind herself to take another. She reached out and brushed a windblown strand of hair from his eyes. "I never expected you either," she said, her voice soft.

"What are we going to do with ourselves?"

"I have no idea. Maybe you could kiss me again and we could figure it out?"

Ronan reached out and grabbed her waist, pulling her toward him. She straddled his legs, her arms wrapped around his neck. His hands skimmed over her shoulders and down her back. And then he pulled her into a kiss, his mouth plundering hers.

It wasn't a kiss meant to tease but one that told her exactly what he wanted from her. There was no reason to question his attraction anymore. And though it may be purely physical, Charlie didn't see anything wrong with that. They were both consenting adults and it had been far too long since she'd been to bed with a man.

His lips traced a path from her mouth to her collarbone and she tipped her head back, her fingers tangled in his hair. Though she'd just met him that morning, they didn't feel like strangers.

His hands slipped beneath her T-shirt, finding naked skin and the sensation of his touch sent a flood of heat racing through her body. If they'd been somewhere more private, Charlie knew that her clothes would have been discarded without a second thought.

She wanted to see his body, to touch the places that were still hidden beneath clothes, to know him in a more intimate way. He was almost too perfect and yet, his desires had overwhelmed him in the same way hers had crushed her inhibitions.

When his palm cupped her breast, a moan slipped from her throat and Charlie knew that resisting him would be impossible. She reached for the hem of his

T-shirt and pulled it over his head, breaking their contact for just an instant.

Her mouth found his again and Charlie let her fingers drift over his shoulders and his back. Though she'd seen him earlier, after his shower, this was different. Touch was much a much more powerful sense than sight. The act of touching his skin was almost more than she could handle.

She'd only been with one man in her life. From the first time he'd kissed her when she was sixteen until the day she'd walked out on him eight years later. They'd learned about sex together and over the years, it hadn't grown more passionate—only more ordinary.

But Ronan Quinn was not an ordinary man. And any intimacy with him would probably be something extraordinary. Would she know how to please him? Were there things that she didn't know?

She'd always been a good actress, always been able to fake her way through almost anything. But sex with a man like Ronan was something that couldn't be faked. He'd know if her need was real.

"Do you think we might be able to find somewhere a bit more comfortable?" he murmured. "Maybe someplace that doesn't rock back and forth?"

She drew back and smiled. "You don't think a smelly oyster boat is comfortable?"

He growled, gently biting at her lower lip. "No."

"Maybe we should go back, then." She crawled off his lap and pulled him to his feet. "You can drive. You have to learn sometime."

Charlie watched as he walked to the bow and pulled

up the anchor. When he sat down next to her, she showed him how to start the boat. A few seconds later, they were back out on the bay, traveling north toward town.

It had been a strange and wonderful day, Charlie thought to herself. That morning, when she crawled out of bed, all she'd had to look forward to was a long day at work. But now, with Ronan around, there were so many more possibilities to consider.

"So how do you feel?" she shouted.

He laughed. "Not good. But I think I'm getting better at hiding it."

3

"I'M SORRY ABOUT dinner," Charlie said. "That chicken was pretty bad."

She set the oyster plate down on the table and sat down next to him, tucking her feet beneath her. Ronan's arm was draped across the back of the wicker sofa and he felt her hair against his skin, a tumble of silken strands.

Every time they made contact he found himself wanting more. He wasn't satisfied to just enjoy a short interlude. Ronan craved endless hours to explore and to touch, to discover everything about her that was sweet and sexy and perfect.

And it wasn't just the touching and the kissing that he craved. He loved to talk to her. It was like she held some secret key to his tongue. He wanted to tell her more about himself, as if she was the only one in the world that might understand him.

How was it possible that a woman like Charlotte Sibley was still single? Did men in this part of the country not find her attractive? Sure, she was strong and resilient and clever. And she walked around in torn jeans and yellow rubber boots. But those were all qualities he found undeniably attractive. And she was also just about the prettiest woman he'd ever met.

After tying up the boat, they'd found a spot on the small terrace outside the tasting room, a spot that overlooked the river. The sun had gone down and the lights from Newcastle twinkled from across the water.

"Hot cottage cheese, curry and chicken was a pretty strange combination. I'm used to lots of different ethnic food, but I've never tasted anything quite like that."

"My mother believes in developing an adventuresome palate in all of her children."

He reached out and picked up an oyster from the plate she'd prepared. "I think I could survive quite nicely on oysters."

"You'll get tired of them sooner or later," she said. "It's like anything you get too much of."

"I can't imagine getting too much of kissing you," he said. Ronan's fingers tangled in her hair and he gently pulled her closer. He was ready to take her to bed, to find out how good they could be together. But he wasn't sure they ought to move so fast. He had six weeks with her. Taking such a big step on their first night together didn't seem like a sensible course of action. Still, if she offered, he wasn't going to refuse.

"I enjoyed meeting your family," he said, taking her hand. "They're so different from mine."

She watched him toy with her fingers as she spoke. "They're different from everyone's family. My mother has always let us go our own way. She wanted us to express our individuality. I think that's really good in theory, but it doesn't always work out in practice. We were known around town as a houseful of hooligans." She shook her head. "That's why I ran away to New York."

"At dinner, your mother mentioned that you lived there."

"I left Sibleyville the day I graduated from high school. With my boyfriend, Danny. We were going to take Broadway by storm. We did all the shows in high school and did a few years of summer stock up in Bar Harbor. Lots of people said we'd be big stars."

"It didn't work out?"

"Not at first. But after three years, things started to click for me. I got a few decent acting jobs. I found an agent. Got my SAG card. But then I had this long dry spell and I decided, if I was going to be miserable, I'd rather be miserable at home, with my family around me."

"Did you like being an actress?"

"I did. I really liked it when I actually got work. But I spent six years going nowhere. And Danny and I weren't getting along, so when I moved out, I came back home for a while. I was just going to stay for a month or two, but then I never went back. When my dad got hurt, I started to run the farm for him." She glanced up at him. "So, that was my big dream. Over by the time I turned twenty-four."

"I'm just impressed that you can sing and dance as well as shuck oysters and drive a boat."

"Yes. And I'm an excellent tap dancer. I actually

got a callback for the revival of Anything Goes. But I didn't get the part."

"But you followed your dream, right?"

"Yeah, but where did it leave me? I didn't go to college. What I should have been doing was getting a business degree."

"Were you in love with him?"

"Danny?" She shook her head. "We were so young. Everyone thought we'd be the ones to break the curse. The first couple from Sibleyville to fall in love and get married. But I'm not sure we ever were in love. We thought we were. We pretended to be in love, but we were just kids with big dreams."

"I'm glad you came back. If you hadn't, I'd still be looking for a job right now. And I'd be sleeping on a park bench."

"Oh, I'm sure some pretty girl would have picked you up and taken you home with her."

A long silence grew between them as that idea hung in the air. Ronan waited, wondering if she'd change her mind and spend the night. He could see the indecision in her expression and decided to help her along. "What time does work start in the morning?"

"Sunrise," she said. Charlie glanced at her watch. "It's almost nine-thirty. I should probably let you get to bed."

She started to rise, but Ronan grabbed her hand and pulled her back down. He gave her one last kiss, his palm smoothing over her cheek as his lips captured hers. "I'd ask you to stay, but I'm not going to do that."

"You shouldn't," she said, breathless, watching him

with wide eyes. "I—I think that would probably be best. I might just agree to stay."

He ran his thumb along her lower lip. "We wouldn't want to move too fast," he said.

"No. Fast is bad," she said. She slowly got to her feet, her fingers still tangled with his. "I'm going to go now. I'll see you in the morning."

"In the morning," Ronan said, standing up beside her. He leaned close and kissed her cheek. "Sleep well."

A tiny laugh bubbled up in her throat. "Right. I'm not sure I'll be doing a lot of sleeping tonight." Charlie drew a deep breath. "I'm going to lock up downstairs. If you decide to leave, you can just use this door and go down the steps from the porch. There's a key on the hook by the door."

"I'll be fine," he said. "I don't think I'll be going anywhere."

"Good," she said. "I'd hate to think we scared you away after only one day."

He didn't want to her leave, which was an odd feeling for Ronan. He was usually the kind of guy who used the "early meeting" excuse to avoid waking up with a woman in his bed. But he'd had such a nice day with Charlotte that he wanted it to go on a little longer.

He stood up and grabbed her hands. "You don't scare me, Charlie."

She shifted nervously, her gaze fixed on his chest. "You kinda scare me, a little bit."

He hooked his thumb beneath her chin and tipped her gaze up to meet his. "We'll have to work on that," he said. "Baby steps."

"I'll see you in the morning," she said.

"All right." He kissed her again, softly, his tongue teasing at the crease of her lips. And when he drew back, he pressed his damp lips to her forehead. "You better go while I'm still willing to let you."

Charlie turned and walked back inside. He watched her in the dim light from the living room lamps and when he heard the door shut behind her, he let out a long breath.

"Charlotte Sibley," he murmured to himself. He leaned against the railing and stared out at the water. What where his brothers doing right now, he wondered. Were they staring out into the night sky and wondering what changes would come over the next six weeks. Had they found an interesting woman to occupy their thoughts?

If he couldn't imagine a different life, here in Sibleyville, with Charlotte Sibley, then he had no imagination at all. This place was perfect, Charlie was beautiful, and there was every chance that they'd be sharing a bed before long.

He'd been drifting for so long, trying to find his place in life. Now, suddenly, he felt the gentle tug of an anchor. The wind might blow and the current might catch him, but he was here to stay, at least for a while. And whatever happened between them, Ronan suspected it might just change his life. And yet he didn't care. His life needed changing, the more, the better. And he'd start with his fear of water.

"Bring it on," he said, taking a sip of his beer. "I'm ready."

THE STREETS WERE silent as Charlie walked home from the boathouse. She'd decided to leave her truck behind, knowing that the exercise and the time to think would give her at least a shot at sleeping.

A soft breeze rustled the trees above her head, the old streetlamps creating strange shadows on the sidewalk in front of her. Though it was late August, she could feel autumn in the air. It was waiting, just a few weeks away, ready to begin turning the trees and chilling the air and making her favorite season of the year come alive again. It would be nice to share it all with someone new.

Since walking out on Danny, she hadn't seriously considered getting involved with a man again. There had been a couple possibilities, but neither of them seemed worth the effort it would take. And there just hadn't been any chemistry.

But Ronan was different. There was something about him that promised excitement and passion and time together that was new and real and special. She felt a tremor course through her body and Charlie rubbed her arms against the goose bumps that prickled her skin.

"Charlotte? Charlotte Sibley, is that you?"

Charlie squinted into the dark and saw a shadowy figure approach with a familiar little dog trotting at her side. Leticia Trowbridge was Sibleyville's chief matchmaker. Ever since the spell was cast, extra help was needed to introduce eligible bachelors to the potential brides and vice versa. The Trowbridge family always provided a spinster relative to take care of the task.

Leticia visited the surrounding towns, looking for

interested mates for the residents. Charlie's mother was introduced to her father by Leticia's great-aunt, the previous matchmaker. Charlie considered turning around and walking in the opposite direction. But Lettie was as tenacious as her little terrier and ignoring her now would make her only more determined,

"Evening, Lettie."

Her little Westie pranced along at her side and Charlie bent down to pet the dog. "Hello, Poppy. How are you tonight?"

"She has a sore paw," Lettie said. "I think she might have stepped on a piece of glass on our morning walk. I'm glad I ran into you, Charlotte."

Charlie had her doubts that their meeting had happened by chance. In truth, she'd been expecting Lettie to show up all evening, ready to evaluate the new man in town, especially since he was a Quinn and sleeping at the Sibley boathouse.

No doubt she knew of Ronan Quinn's arrival just minutes after it happened. Maxine at the visitor's center had Lettie on speed dial. She'd probably already done a background check, a credit check and a Google search, preparing a file that would rival those of the Secret Service.

"I'm just on my way home, Lettie. I've had a really long day."

"I know! And that's exactly what I wanted to talk to you about. I hear we have a new man in town. And he's single and handsome and will be working for you."

"All of that is correct," she said. "And he's a Quinn."

"You know what this means, don't you?"

Charlie sighed and ran her fingers through her wind-blown hair. "I really don't think he's going to want to be set up on any dates, Lettie. He's only here for six weeks and then he's heading back to Seattle. So he won't have time to date. You can ask him, but I think he'll agree."

"I'm not thinking of him for my other clients. I'm thinking of him for you, Charlotte."

"Me?" Charlie shook her head. "No, no, no. He's my employee. You are not going to bother him with any of your manipulations. Especially if they're on my behalf. I'm not interested in getting married."

"Don't you understand, Charlotte? If you fall in love with this man and marry him, the curse will be broken. He's a Quinn, you're a Sibley. It's meant to be. After all these years, the marriage that Bridie wanted can happen."

"Shhh! Lettie, please. Don't start with this. I'm not interested in marrying Ronan. We don't even know each other. Besides, he lives in Seattle."

Lettie wagged her finger at Charlie. "Let me be very clear here, Charlotte. The entire town is depending on you. We've lived with this curse for far too long. And I've been thinking about retiring to Florida for the last three years only I've been stuck here trying to fix people up so that at least a few of our citizens can find a happily-ever-after. I'm tired. I want to spend my days playing shuffleboard and my nights playing canasta with my sister, Prudy."

What was she supposed to say? If Ronan got wind of Lettie's plans, he'd be on the next bus out of town. "How many people have you told about this?" Charlie asked.

"No one. I wanted to talk to you first."

"All right. I want to keep it that way. There's no use getting the whole town all excited about something that might never happen."

Charlie knew she'd need to buy herself some time. If she could convince Lettie to keep her plans to herself, maybe she might manage to save herself some embarrassment. After all, she had no intention of marrying Ronan Quinn! Maybe she'd fool around a little with him, but in six weeks, he'd return to Seattle and she'd go on with her life in Sibleyville.

"I'm going to need all the advice you can give me. But you cannot tell my mother about this. We're going to have to meet secretly. I'll let you know how things are going, you can tell me what I need to do to close the deal."

Lettie took a moment to mull over this request before she nodded. "All right. But first, tell me everything you know about him. I need to know exactly what we're up against."

"This is going to have to wait until tomorrow. Maybe I could stop by your house and we could talk?"

"Fine," Lettie said. She drew Charlie into a fierce hug. "We're going to do this together. We're going to make him fall madly in love with you and then we're going to break this horrid curse. I'm going to be the Trowbridge that brings love back to Sibleyville." She giggled softly and started off down the street, Poppy beside her. "I may just write a book about it."

As if she wasn't having enough trouble maintaining her composure around Ronan, now she'd have Lettie looking over her shoulder, questioning her every move. Charlie always knew that when it came time to find a man, she'd find one on her own, without outside help. After all, she really didn't believe in the curse.

She drew a deep breath of the night air, the scent of salt drifting up from the river. As she approached her parents' house, she noticed that it was ablaze with light. It looked like everyone was still up.

She slowly climbed the front steps, then noticed her mother, sitting on the porch swing, a cool drink in her hand. Charlie wandered over and sat down beside her. They rocked back and forth for a long time, neither one of them saying anything.

"Dinner was good," Charlie said.

Her mother took her hand and gave it a pat. "You're a sweet daughter," she said. "But I don't need you to lie to me. It was pretty awful. I'm just sorry that your new friend had to suffer through it."

Charlie wrapped her arm around her mother's and rested her head on her shoulder. "He didn't mind. We had oysters later."

"He seems like a nice young man."

"Yes, mother, he is a very nice young man." Her mind flashed back to the kisses they'd shared, to the feel of his hands on her body, to the wild sensations that raced through her at his touch. He was also a very bad boy.

"Handsome, too."

"Ummmm-hmmmm."

"How long before you think Lettie will come calling?"

"She met me on the street on my way home. She thinks we should get married and that will break the curse." Charlie drew back. "You and daddy met through the matchmaker, didn't you?"

"Well, not really. We knew each other before that. She just suggested that we give it a go. And we did. I liked him as much the second time I met him as I did the first. What girl wouldn't love him?"

"I'm not sure I want to fall in love," Charlie said.

"Why not?"

"I can't imagine wanting to spend my whole entire life with the same person."

"That's your problem, Charlotte. You can't imagine it. When the right man comes along, it doesn't require any thought or imagination. You'll just know and it will be right."

"You're very smart," Charlie teased.

"Did I ever tell you how glad we are to have you home? I don't know what we'd do without you now that your dad is laid up."

"I'm happy to help, Mom. I like working the farm."

"But if I ever get the sense that you're just hiding out here, to avoid making the difficult choices, I'm going to have to kick you right back out of the nest. You need to go out into the world and make your dreams come true. And if it doesn't happen the first time, then you keep trying until it does happen."

Charlie kissed her mother's cheek. "Yes, Mom." She stood up. "I need a long, hot shower and then I'm going to bed."

"You're going to have a hard day at work tomorrow," he mother said.

"Yes, I am."

"Spending all that time and energy trying not to fall for Ronan Quinn. I suspect it will be exhausting."

It already was, Charlie thought to herself.

FOR THE FIRST time in four days, Ronan had gotten a full night's sleep. No more uncomfortable bus seats or noisy children or bumpy highways. He now had the luxury of a lovely queen size bed in an apartment overlooking the water.

He'd turned off the air-conditioning, thrown open the window and drifted off to the sounds of the river. But his internal clock, reset during his bus drive, woke him in time to see the sun just peeking over the horizon.

Ronan crawled out of bed, wearing only his boxers, and rubbed his arms against the damp chill in the air. The kitchen had basic supplies and after a quick search, he found coffee, filters and the coffee maker. By the time the coffee was filling the pot, he was waiting with a mug.

Wisps of steam drifted up from the mug as he stepped out onto the terrace. The commercial boats that tied up along the docks in Sibleyville were already up and running. Though he was about to start his first day of work at the Mistry Bay Oyster Farm, Ronan wasn't thinking about the job. His mind was firmly fixed on his boss.

He'd never had close friends. When he needed someone's advice or company, he always relied on his brothers. And when it came to women, he'd always held them at a careful distance. But with Charlotte Sibley, Ronan felt like he could have both—a friend and a lover. That had never happened before and he wasn't sure how to handle it.

Should they solidify their friendship first and then indulge in physical pleasures? Or would the physical intimacies make for a deeper friendship. Ronan was at a loss when it came to his next step. All he knew was that he needed to spend more time with Charlie. A lot more time.

He heard a knock at the front door of the apartment and Ronan strode back inside and grabbed a pair of jeans, tugging them on before he continued to the door. When he opened it, the object of his early morning fantasies was standing in the hallway, her hair still damp from her shower. She clutched a bag in her hand and had tucked a thermos under her arm.

"Morning," she said, stepping inside. "Did you sleep well?"

"Like a baby," Ronan said, grinning at her. "How about you?"

"Not a wink," she muttered. She quickly turned to face him. "Listen, we need to set some ground rules. I was up all last night just thinking about kissing you and—"

"You were?" Ronan slipped his arms around her waist. "What were you thinking about?"

She backed away from him and walked to the table. "If we're going to...you know...mess around, then we need to do it outside of work. I can't focus on the job if all I'm thinking about is you." She paused and glanced up at him. "Can we do that?"

"Sure," he said.

She released a tightly held breath and nodded. "All right. Then grab a shirt. We'll get you a pair of waders and some boots. Do you have a sweater or a jacket?"

"Nothing I can wear on a boat," he said.

"Come on, then," Charlie said. "I'll get you what you need."

Five minutes later, they were downstairs, rummaging through his wardrobe choices. When he'd been outfitted in a fleece jacket, gloves, rubber waders and boots, they headed out to the dock. Charlie jumped into the skiff and pointed to the stern line. "Grab that one," she said as she crawled to the bow.

He did as he was told, but when it came time to jump into the boat, Ronan hesitated. She looked up at him. "Take your time," she said.

"Right." He nodded, then began to slowly pace back and forth on the pier. "I don't know why this is giving me a problem. I think the water just looks…darker."

She reached into the bag she'd carried and pulled out a donut. "Bearclaw?" she asked.

Ronan shook his head. Right now, anything he ate was guaranteed to come right back up again. "Baby steps," he murmured.

She nodded and took a bite, slowly chewing as she watched him from the boat. Cursing softly, he drew a deep breath and jumped into the skiff. His head slammed in his chest and he felt a familiar rush of panic.

But he wasn't going to let it overwhelm him. "All right," he murmured. "Let's go."

True to their arrangement, she was keeping everything very professional, including her attitude toward him. He needed a kiss, a touch, anything to distract his thoughts. He knew if he pulled her into his arms, she'd relent and respond. But he could certainly control his impulses—at least for the next eight to ten hours.

His thoughts, however, were an entirely different matter. She couldn't keep him from enjoying a vivid fantasy during the workday. And though baggy waders and faded fleece jacket weren't the height of sexy attire, Ronan didn't care. He liked the way she looked, all tough and ready to meet the elements.

As she maneuvered away from the dock and into the river, he felt a sliver of fear, but focused his mind on a careful study of her features, outlined by the soft light of the sunrise.

"Here," she said, stepping away. "Take the wheel. Just stay to the center of the channel."

He did as ordered, sliding into the seat behind the controls. Charlie opened the thermos, then grabbed a pair of mugs from a locker beneath her seat. She handed him a mug, the poured one for herself.

"Thanks," he said. "Maybe I should try one of those donuts. It might settle my stomach."

She opened the bag and held it out to him. "Bearclaw. Breakfast of champions."

Ronan chuckled. He set the mug on a nearby ledge and grabbed the pastry, taking a huge bite. "Oh, God, it's still warm."

She nodded as she bit into her breakfast. "Yeah. You can't go wrong. There's a bakery just down the street from the boathouse. They open at five a.m. Sunrise is at six these days, so there's always something coming out of the oven."

He stared at her for a long moment, then turned to look out over the water. "This is going to be pretty tricky," he said.

"Just follow the buoys," she said. "Keep the red on your left and the green on your right as we're going out to sea. And then, the opposite as we're coming in. Red on the left, going on the right, returning. Just remember that."

"That's not what I was talking about," Ronan said.

"What were you talking about?"

"I was thinking about how difficult it would be to keep from kissing you. You look beautiful this morning," he said.

Charlie laughed, the sound echoing over the water and through the early morning mist. "Oh, please."

"You do. I really like the outfit. I know it sounds crazy, but it's taking all my strength not to grab you and have my way with you."

"Eat your bearclaw," she said with a coy smile. "And you are full of it, by the way. Any man who thinks this is sexy is sick, sick, sick."

Maybe that was it, Ronan mused. Maybe this was some kind of physical malady that would disappear with a few days rest. Whenever he was close to her, he did feel a little feverish.

"So, boss, what are we doing today?"

"We're going to stop by the nursery and pick up some crates of seed oysters and then we're going to plant them in the bay."

"How do we do that?"

"It's a very complicated technique," she said. "We put on our snorkel gear and jump in the water and take each little oyster and plant it in a perfect row on the bottom of the bay."

"Really?"

"No. Weren't you listening last night? I think I explained it."

Ronan groaned. "I had other things on my mind. Maybe you should go over it again."

She laughed at him and the sound was sweet and musical. He'd never known any woman who could make him smile as much as Charlie could. Nothing ever seemed to bother her. Maybe he'd just dated the wrong women, Ronan thought to himself, somber, depressing women who never smiled or laughed. Was this what a relationship was supposed to be like—light and teasing and fun?

"Wait, let me see if I can find my notes," Ronan said. "I was taking notes, wasn't I?"

"All right, I'll explain once more, but pay attention."

His gaze skimmed her pretty features and he nodded.

"You're going to carefully take a shovel full of oysters and you're going to toss them over the side as I'm driving the boat very slowly over the beds. They're going to sink to the bottom and stay there for a few years, until we're ready to harvest them. We have two more days of planting, then we have to start harvesting some of the mature beds."

"How do you make sure you get the oysters that are ready?"

"We plant the bay in sections. This season we'll harvest the section that we planted a few years ago."

He poked at his forehead with his gloved finger. "Got it. I won't forget that."

She reached over and ruffled his hair. It was such an innocent gesture, but it said everything about the two of them. After only a day, they were completely comfortable with each other. He didn't have to think about what he said before he said it. She was so open and honest, not the kind of girl who played games.

She looked out over the water, then pointed to one of the red buoys. "Watch out," she warned.

He changed direction, then took another bite of his bearclaw. Right now, Ronan couldn't imagine wanting to be any other place in the world. For a guy who never felt like he belonged, this was exactly where he needed to be for the moment. And maybe for longer than that.

4

THE AFTERNOON SUN beat down on the skiff and Charlie slowly maneuvered the boat along a line running parallel to the shore. Ronan stood in the open bow, his jacket and shirt discarded, his tanned body gleaming with perspiration.

He'd started the day uneasy about being on the water. Charlie had seen the look of panic in his eyes whenever she caught him looking down into the dark water. But she'd advised him to keep his eyes on the horizon and that seemed to calm his fears.

Though she'd barely known him a day, she couldn't help but wonder about the complex man who stood before her. He seemed invincible, yet flawed. Strong, yet sensitive. Engaged yet indifferent in many ways. Though he admitted that he felt most comfortable when he was alone, she'd found him to be a clever conversationalist, when he felt like talking.

Ronan gently scooped up a shovel full of seed oysters and then, in a wide sweeping motion, tossed them into the water. Charlie had showed him the technique earlier and it had taken him only a few tries before he understood what she needed.

She watched the play of muscle across his back and a tiny shiver of desire skittered through her. If this was what she'd have to put up with every day, then keeping her hands off of Ronan was going to be nearly impossible. She couldn't keep her eyes off him, either. He was standing there, right in front of her, like some beautiful statue made of flesh and bone instead of cold marble.

"What do you have left up there?" she called as she brought the boat around. Her voice wavered slightly and she cleared her throat.

An image flashed in her mind and she brushed it aside. If her mind insisted on removing the rest of his clothes, then she had no choice but to think about other things. "Oysters," she muttered to herself. "Oysters."

"Maybe five or six more tosses," he called.

"Let me go down to the south end. We can push that a little further out, I think." She watched her depth finder as she navigated to the spot.

Buoys marked off the different areas of the bay and the oysters were scattered in carefully drawn areas, chosen for optimum growing conditions. Charlie knew the bay like the back of her hand, the shoreline, the depths, the muddy flats and the spots where the current ran strong.

"How much of this water is yours?" Ronan asked, bracing his arm on the shovel handle.

"None of it is ours. We lease it from the state. We own the land on Kepley Pond where the hatchery is, but none of this."

Charlie found the spot she wanted and called to him and Ronan finished the last of the seed oysters. After setting the shovel down, he made his way back to Charlie, flopping down on the seat next to her. "Do we have another load to do?"

They'd gone back to the hatchery twice already that day. "Nope. We're finished."

He raised his hands above his head and shouted. "All right! I survived." Ronan turned to her and slipped his arm around her shoulder, pulling her into a long, deep kiss. When he drew back, he had a devilish smile on his face. "Wait. Did I jump the gun? Do I have to wait until we dock at the boathouse?"

"No," she said. "Work is officially over. You did well. How do you feel?"

"Exhausted. There were times when I just wanted off this boat, but I tried to focus on the job and that helped." He kissed her again, tossing off his gloves so he could cup her face in his hands. "Thanks for being so patient with me. Can we drive home closer to the shore?"

"It'll take us longer," she said.

"I'm good with that."

He kissed her again, so sweet and so gentle, yet there was a raw power to his kiss that promised so much more. Charlie found it impossible to resist him. She was, after just a day, completely infatuated with the man.

She'd always considered herself a fairly sensible person when it came to romance. With Danny, everything had been simple and straight-forward. But this romance was completely the opposite, a maelstrom of intense and uncontrollable feelings.

The urge to toss aside her inhibitions and totally surrender to Ronan was becoming more and more difficult to ignore. She wanted to laugh out loud and leap through fields of daisies and sing love songs at the top of her voice. The old Charlotte Sibley would have been mortified to caught doing anything so ridiculous. But Charlie didn't care what other people thought. The only thing she cared about was the man sitting next to her.

"What are we going to do tonight?" he murmured, his breath soft against her ear.

She smoothed her hands across his chest and drew back. "Do you want to do anything? I thought you might want to relax. You're going to be sore tomorrow."

"I'm in good shape," he said. "I won't be sore."

"You will be. Believe me, unless you make a living shoveling snow, you're going to feel it. The first time I did that job, I couldn't move for three days."

He chuckled. "That's because you're a girl," he said with a shrug.

Charlie gasped. "You did not just say that."

He winced. "Backsies," Ronan said. An odd look suddenly came over his face and he turned away.

"Backsies? What is that?"

He laughed softly. "I don't know where that came from. It was buried really deep. Twenty years deep."

"What is it?"

He turned back to her and forced a smile. "My mom used to say that. Whenever one of us would say something nasty, she'd ask if we wanted a backsie, which meant we could take it back before anyone heard it. It was her way of making us think before we spoke."

"You don't have to take it back. I knew you were teasing." She turned her gaze to meet his. "Are you all right?"

"Yeah," he said. "It was a nice memory." Ronan drew a deep breath. "Are we having dinner with your folks again?"

Charlie shook her head. "No, we don't have to."

"What cuisine is it tonight?"

"Most of the time we have normal food," she explained. "Maybe meatloaf or roasted chicken or pork chops. Mona's really a pretty decent cook. And once a month we have Thanksgiving."

"Thanksgiving?"

Charlie nodded. "My mother thinks that a meal so wonderful should be enjoyed more than once a year. So she makes a turkey and dressing and mashed potatoes and all the fixings. We eat off my great-grandmother's china and use the Sibley silver. And everyone has to be there. I think we're having Thanksgiving next week."

"That sounds pretty wonderful," he said. "We never really celebrated Thanksgiving, at least not after my folks died. My grandfather is from Ireland and he didn't quite understand the tradition."

"What are you in the mood for tonight?" she asked.

"Can we eat raw oysters and drink beer again?"

"You can. I'll order Thai food. But before we do anything, you're going to need to take a shower. You smell like oysters."

"You don't smell like a rose garden yourself," he said, hugging her close. He drew a deep breath, his face buried in her windswept hair. "Nope, no roses there."

Charlie's cellphone rang and she reached into her waders and pulled it from her jacket pocket. The caller I.D. said "Isaac." "Hey, what's up? Where are you?"

"I got a call from Uncle Jake," Isaac said. "They lost a dredging basket when the line broke so we came over to see if we could snag it. Abs and I are diving for it, but we're getting a little cold. Should we leave it and come back with scuba gear tomorrow?"

"No, let me give it a try. You're across from Palmer Cove?"

"Yep," Isaac said.

"Be there in about ten minutes." Charlie put her phone back in her pocket. "We have to give Isaac a hand. It'll only take a few minutes. Then we'll head back to the boathouse."

She turned the skiff toward the mouth of the bay and hit the throttle. From end to end, Mistry Bay was nearly forty miles long. Work crews from the farm were often on the bay at the same time, yet rarely saw each other. She found her siblings across from the cove they'd been seeding, their skiff bobbing on the water. Abby and Isaac were huddled in the boat.

Charlie maneuvered the skiff next to theirs and tied it up at the bow and stern. "How deep is it?"

"About fifteen feet," Isaac said. "I had it once, but my knot slipped. Without a mask, I couldn't really see. It's full of oysters." He looked over at Ronan. "Charlie is the best diver in the family."

Ronan stared at her, his mouth agape. "You're going to jump in the water?"

Charlie nodded. "Don't worry. I've done this lots of times."

"She sometimes harvests oysters by diving," Abby said. "She can hold her breath longer than anyone in the family. Almost two minutes."

Kicking off her rubber boots, Charlie slipped the straps of her waders over her shoulders and stepped out of them. Her jacket came next and then her jeans. When she was down to her panties and her T-shirt, she stepped to the stern of the boat.

"Wait a minute," Ronan said. "Is this really necessary? I'll buy you a new basket."

"We don't want to lose equipment." She motioned to Isaac. "Hand me the line." She wrapped the rope around her waist and knotted it, then dove over the side.

The bottom of the bay was mud and unlike sand, it didn't reflect the light. But Charlie saw the dredge right away and swam over to it. She unwrapped the line from her waist and then, taking her time, tied it through the bracket, making sure the knot was tight. She grabbed an oyster from the bottom, then kicked for the surface.

Ronan was waiting, staring over the stern with a worried expression. He held out his hand and helped her into the skiff, then wrapped his jacket around her shoulders and rubbed her back. "Are you all right?"

"Yeah." She held out the oyster to him. "I brought you a present."

"An oyster?"

"The freshest oyster you've ever eaten," she said. "Come on, I'll open it for you."

Isaac and Abby had managed to drag the basket into the boat. "What do you want to do with these?"

"Take half home to Mom. She can make oyster stew. And leave about half of them at the boathouse. Ronan needs dinner."

Isaac untied his boat from Charlie's skiff and a few seconds later, he and Abby were skimming across the water toward the main channel. Ronan stared down at her, wiping the water from her face.

"That scared the crap out of me," he said. "Don't ever do that again."

"It's not that deep. And there's nothing down there to hurt me. I'll show you. Next time we have a low tide, we'll walk out here and harvest by hand."

He frowned. "You can do that?"

She pushed up on her toes and kissed him. "You have a lot to learn about oyster farming, rookie."

Ronan growled softly and pulled her into a fierce embrace. "I think I have a lot to learn about you, Charlotte Sibley," he said, before his mouth found hers again.

A LONG HOT shower was the perfect end to a hard day at work. Ronan had never felt this pleasant kind of exhaustion after a day of working at the yachtworks. Maybe it was all the fresh air or the intense labor, but every muscle in his body had been taxed.

He'd slipped into a pair of cargo shorts and then wandered out into the kitchen. To his surprise, the refrigerator had been stocked with food and drink sometime during the day. The cupboard above the sink also held a variety of snacks. Had Charlie done this?

He found the answer on a note in a basket of fresh fruit. Penny Sibley. Charlie's mother. He grabbed a beer from the fridge and twisted it open.

His stomach growled. They'd had a quick lunch of ham sandwiches at the hatchery, but nothing since then. "Oysters," he murmured.

Somewhere in this building were the oysters Isaac and Abby had pulled out of the bay. He grabbed the front door, but as he pulled it open, he found Charlie standing on the other side.

She held a paper bag, a plastic bucket of oysters and a six-pack of beer. "Help," she said. "Grab the bag."

The scent of Thai spices drifted through the air. "I was just going to search out those oysters."

"I brought these from home," she said. "My mom had cleaned them and set them aside for you."

"She stocked my refrigerator, too," Ronan said, stepping aside so Charlie could enter.

Charlie turned to face him, her surprise etched across her beautiful face. "She did? Well, that was very nice of her. She's taken a liking to you." She set the beer on the counter, then began to unpack the Thai food from the bag. But since she'd walked in, Ronan had suddenly forgotten all about food. He was hungry for Charlie instead.

He'd spent the entire day observing her, reveling in each new detail he discovered. Unlike other women he'd known, Charlie wasn't afraid to get her hands dirty. She worked a job that took strength and patience and insight. Her body wasn't toned by a trainer, but by hard, physical work. Her day began at dawn and ended when the work was done. She was a remarkable woman.

Ronan stood behind her and wrapped his arms around her waist. She smelled like citrus. He drew a deep breath and closed his eyes. "Leave the food," he said.

"You're not hungry?"

Ronan grabbed the bucket of oysters and put them in the fridge, then turned her around to face him. He grabbed her waist and set her on the edge of the counter. "God, you smell good. And you're so damn pretty."

"This is going to get out of hand," she warned, smoothing his hair away from his forehead. "You can't keep telling me I'm pretty. And you have to stop smelling my hair."

"Is that so bad? We managed to keep our hands off each other all day today."

With a groan, Charlie pulled him into a kiss. But this time, Ronan felt that the kiss was just a prelude to something more.

She ran her hands over his naked chest, her palms warm against his skin, her fingernails raking across his shoulders. It had been awhile since he'd been touched like this and Ronan felt an instant response. He stepped between her legs, wrapping them around his waist.

Ronan lost himself in the taste of her mouth, in the feel of her caress on his body. In one way, they were still strangers, unaware of the pleasures they could bring each other. But in just one day, he felt as if he knew her better than he'd ever known any another woman.

Ronan reached for the front of her shirt and slowly

brushed it over her shoulders, revealing the pretty cami-sole beneath. His lips traced a path from her mouth to her neck, the intoxicating scent of her skin making his body pulse with need.

He wanted to rush, to tear off their clothes and bury himself in her warmth. He needed to know how far she'd go. This wasn't some one-night stand, fueled by too many drinks and a need for release.

He'd found a woman who was more than just a beautiful face and a willing and warm body. He liked Charlie. He felt the need to protect her from anything that might hurt her. Ronan knew it the moment she'd jumped off the boat to retrieve that dredging basket. She was clever and resourceful—and fearless.

Ronan slipped his hands beneath her backside and picked her up, carrying her into the bedroom. He laid her on the bed and stretched out above her, their mouths still lost in a passionate kiss. Charlie pulled him down on top of her, wriggling until his hips fit perfectly against hers.

"I thought you were hungry," she murmured.

"There are some things more important than food," Ronan replied. He rolled to his side and drew back, taking in the perfect details of her face.

When he smoothed her hair out of her eyes, she looked up at him. "Don't stop," she murmured.

Ronan shrugged. "I won't. It feels too good."

Her lips curled into a smile and she nodded. "I've only ever been with one man," she said. "And we started dating when we were in high school. I'm not sure I know how to do this. Like a grown-up."

He ran his hand along her hip and slid it beneath her camisole. "There's no instruction book, Charlie," he said. "And they don't teach this in school. We just have to figure it out as we go along."

"Then tell me how to start," she said.

"We've already started," he said. Ronan pulled her into another kiss, his hand slipping beneath her shirt. He found the silky fabric of her bra and gently pulled it aside, cupping the soft flesh of her breast in his hand.

Charlie moaned softly as his thumb grazed her nipple. Her lips were parted slightly and her eyes were closed. Pleasure suffused her expression and she shifted beside him, arching into his touch.

In the end, it was enough to just touch her and kiss her. Though Ronan would have been happy to strip off their clothes and make love to her, he was willing to leave that for another time. He knew what he wanted and it was pretty clear that Charlie wanted the same.

The day had been long and busy for both of them and as they continued to kiss and touch each other, Ronan felt exhaustion suffusing his body. He yawned, then quickly covered his mouth. "That wasn't you," he murmured.

"Close your eyes," she said. "Let's just lie here for a few minutes and wait for our second wind."

"Are you tired, too?"

"Hmmm. I had to do my work and admire you at the same time. That takes a lot out of a girl." She nuzzled her face into his chest. "You looked really nice in those waders. Especially when you took your shirt off."

"And here I thought you were concentrating on your navigation."

"I could do that job in my sleep."

"I like it," Ronan said. "The work. I really do."

She pushed up on her elbow. "Yeah?"

"It's exhausting, but there's something about it that makes it satisfying. You're growing something that people can eat. Something really good to eat. I build yachts for rich people. People who really don't need yachts."

"But they're really beautiful yachts," she said.

"How do you know?"

"Lettie Trowbridge checked you out on Google and she left me a file with all sorts of pictures. I really liked the one you built for that senator from Oregon."

"Really? That was one of my favorites, too." He paused. "Who is Lettie Trowbridge?"

"The town busybody," Charlie said. "Everyone is talking about you. Because you're a Quinn."

"Maybe she was just watching out for you and your family. That's what's nice about a small town. Everyone takes care of everyone else."

"No," Charlie said, shaking her head. "Everyone is in everyone else's business. Do you want to know the truth about Lettie's motives? And the reason that my mother filled your refrigerator? They want you to stay. They want you to marry me so the curse will be broken. They're going to do everything they can to make me and Sibleyville look like paradise on earth. My mother even cleaned those oysters for you. She never cleans oysters."

The words had just tumbled out. He smoothed his

fingers along her jaw line. "I'm thinking you might want a backsie on that whole last rant."

Charlie grew silent, her brow furrowed, her lips pursed. "Okay. Pretend you didn't hear that."

Ronan leaned over her, teasing at the crease between her lips with his tongue. "They really want me to marry you?"

"If a Sibley marries a Quinn, it will break the curse. Lettie wants to retire to Florida. Did I tell you that she's the town matchmaker? If she can't make a match between the two of us, she's going to hook you up with some other girl in town. She has a whole list of Sibley descendants just waiting."

Ronan pressed his finger to her lips. "Shh. Don't let it bother you. I'm sure I can fight them off. I'll just tell them there's only one Sibley I'm interested in."

She sighed softly as she curled into his body. Maybe this was paradise on earth, Ronan thought, drawing her closer.

If it wasn't, it sure came close.

CHARLIE OPENED HER EYES. The room was dark and for a moment, she didn't know where she was. When the body beside her moved, she drew in a sharp breath. But then she remembered she was with Ronan. They'd fallen asleep in his bed.

What time was it? She glanced over her shoulder and squinted at the bedside table. It was just past two in the morning. They'd been asleep for six hours. Charlie sat up and ran her fingers through her hair. She ought to get up and go home, but she had to be up again in about four hours for work.

She bent over and touched her lips to his shoulder. He was lying on his stomach, sprawled across the bed, his breathing deep and even. "Ronan. Ronan, wake up." She gave him a shake and he groaned.

Ronan rolled to his side, then sat up. "We fell asleep. What time is it?"

"Past two. I have to go."

He reached out and rested his hand on her shoulder, his fingers tangling in her hair. "No," he said.

Charlie leaned into him and dropped a kiss on his lips. But he pulled her close again and drew her into a deeper, more desperate kiss. A groan slipped from her throat and she felt her resolve waver.

She'd lost her ability to resist. She'd known this man for two days and she was already in full surrender mode. Even though her instincts told her to be careful, the feelings racing through her body told her otherwise.

They'd found each other in this crazy, loveless town and he was sweet and sexy and everything she might want in a lover. She didn't care that he'd be gone in six weeks. She didn't care that they barely knew each other. Who knew when she'd have another chance like this? She'd been living in Sibleyville for almost a year and handsome, eligible men had been nonexistent.

Charlie reached for the hem of her camisole and pulled it up, breaking their kiss only to draw it over her head. She'd made her intentions clear, but it was up to Ronan to make the next move. He grabbed her hand and helped her off the bed and when they stood beside it, he cupped her face in his hands and pressed his forehead to hers.

"I can wait," he murmured. "This doesn't have to happen tonight."

"No," Charlie said, her voice wavering. "I can't wait." She unzipped her jeans and slid them over her hips, then kicked them aside. She was twenty-five years old and she'd known the touch of just one man. There were passions inside of her, raw and unfamiliar, that she wanted to explore.

Charlie took his hand and placed it on her breast. He drew a deep breath, his gaze still fixed on hers. Slowly, his touch drifted over the swell of flesh. She closed her eyes as he worked at the clasp of her bra and when it fell away, she knew that they'd reached the point of no return.

She'd always known that another man would come into her life, but when she'd pictured the intimate moments, Charlie had always felt a bit of hesitation. Would she know what to do? Would she please him?

With Ronan, there was no fear or doubt. He liked her exactly the way she was. Emboldened to act, she reached for the waistband of his cargo shorts and unbuttoned them. Only after they fell to his feet did she realize that he wasn't wearing boxers.

"Sorry," he murmured.

She reached out and smoothed her hand along his stiff shaft. He was hard and ready and more beautiful than she'd ever imagined. Charlie felt like she was living in the middle of a fantasy, every sensation more overwhelming than the last, making it impossible to think.

But she didn't need to think. She just needed to act. Drawing a ragged breath, she wrapped her fingers around him. Ronan groaned as she began to stroke him. But he wasn't content to let her control the pace of the seduction.

He grabbed her waist and pulled her over to the bed and when she was stretched out in front of him, he drew her panties down her legs and tossed them aside.

Suddenly, his touch was everywhere, his lips exploring her body, his hands gently moving over her curves and angles. Wave after wave of exquisite sensation washed over her with every new spot that he found. The base of her neck, the small of her back, the soft skin behind each knee.

Charlie felt like some erotic goddess, not an inexperienced 25-year old oyster farmer. Every intimacy was a revelation, a beautiful discovery. She'd never felt such intense desire. And when Ronan gently parted her thighs and kissed the damp folds between her legs, the need in her exploded.

Her fingers clutched the sheets as his tongue flicked at her sex. She wanted to stop, to enjoy the foreplay, but her body was at the mercy of his tongue. Like a rogue wave, her orgasm built, growing more powerful with each moment that passed. Pleasure had become a giant wall of water—she felt it surround her, overwhelm her, steal her breath from her lungs.

And then, the wave broke, dissolving in a rush around her. Charlie's body shuddered uncontrollably and she cried out, twisting beneath his assault.

It seemed to last forever, the exquisite pleasure making her fingers and toes tingle. As her pulse slowed and her breath returned, she opened her eyes. He was lying on his back, a satisfied smile on his face.

"What?" she said, resting her hand on his head.

"Oops," he said.

She pushed up on her elbows. "What?"

"I don't think that's happened to me since the first time a girl touched me." He pointed to a wet spot on the bedspread. "I kind of lost control. You were just so…incredible"

Charlie laughed. "I was incredible?"

"Ummm."

"Oops," she said. "I'd offer you a backsie on that, but I don't think that would work."

He growled softly as he crawled up beside her. "There's plenty more where that came from," he said. "Just give me a few minutes."

Charlie swung her legs off the bed. "I know exactly what you need." She walked out into the kitchen and found her shirt, then pulled it on over her naked body. Ronan followed her, the sheet wrapped around his waist.

"What are you doing?"

"Getting us something to eat. I'm starving and you were starving before you dragged me off to bed." She grabbed the bucket of fresh oysters from the refrigerator, then found an oyster knife in the drawer. "Do you think you can handle that without cutting a major artery?"

"Show me how to do it again."

Charlie grabbed a kitchen towel and set it down on the granite peninsula. "Hold it like this, stick the knife into the joint and then just twist." They oyster popped open and she cut out the meat and handed him the shell.

Ronan slurped the oyster down and sighed. "Perfect."

She grabbed a couple of plates and opened the cartons of Thai food. The noodles were cold, but Charlie liked them that way. She dumped some shrimp pad thai onto a plate and sat down across the counter from Ronan.

"Good food and great sex," Ronan said. "What more do I need?"

"Sleep," she said. "We have to be up for work in about three and a half hours."

He groaned, then held out a shucked oyster. She tipped her head back as he fed it to her, the delicacy sliding down her throat. "Umm," she said. "That was a good one."

"I'm kind of looking forward to work," he said as he continued to shuck the oysters. "I had fun yesterday. It was hard work, but it was nice to be outside. And I never thought I'd like being on the water, but…I think I'm going to be all right. It's going to take some time, but I felt like I could breathe out there."

"There are oyster farms in the Pacific Northwest," Charlie said. "When you go home, maybe you could take a job there. Or start your own oyster farm."

He slurped another oyster, then shrugged. "Or maybe I won't go home at all," he said. "Maybe I'll stay here."

Her heart stopped for a moment and then Charlie realized she must have heard him wrong. What exactly was he saying? He couldn't know Sibleyville well enough to make that kind of decision. Was he thinking about staying because of her? "If you're really interested in oyster farming, I could teach you all I know," she said. "There might be some differences out west, but there shouldn't be many."

"I'd like to learn more," he said. "But only during work hours. The rest of my time, I want to spend learning everything I can about you."

She shook her head. "There's not that much to know," Charlie said.

"I'll tell you something about you that you don't know," he said.

She regarded him with a dubious look. "All right."

"You don't have any idea how amazing you are," he said. "I've known a lot of women and not one of them as been as honest and direct as you. Everything that you say is real and true and I don't have to try to figure out what you really mean. You don't play any silly games."

"What kind of women have you been dating?" she asked.

"The wrong kind," he said.

"I don't know how to be that kind of woman," Charlie said. "I never learned. I mean, I'm a decent actress, so I can pretend, but—"

"No, don't do that," Ronan said. "You'd be like every other woman I've known." She rose up and leaned over the counter and he gave her another oyster, then wiped her bottom lip with his thumb. "I never expected you."

"I didn't expect you, either."

"I have no idea where this is going to go."

She shrugged. "Neither do I. But it's going to be fun finding out, don't you think?"

Ronan nodded. "So, are we going to do this every night? Is this going to cause problems with your family?"

"I ran away to New York with my high school boyfriend when I was eighteen. I'm pretty much considered a sexual rebel around Sibleyville." She held out a forkful of noodles and he grabbed the bite. "Besides, everyone in town wants us to get married so we'll break the curse. Believe me, they'll be more than happy that we're sleeping together."

He sent her a wicked grin. "All right then. I think it's our civic duty to make the citizens of Sibleyville happy." Ronan slid off the stool and slowly circled the counter. "I think I'm ready to continue now."

"I'm still eating," she teased.

He took the carton from Charlie's hand and set it down, then drew her along to the bedroom. "We only have three hours until we have to be up for work. I think we need to get started right now."

Charlie slipped out of his grasp and ran to the bedroom, then jumped into the center of the bed. He followed her, throwing the sheet off at the last minute.

He retrieved a box of condoms from his bag, then pulled her along with him as they tumbled onto the mattress. Ronan settled himself between her legs and caught her in a long and passionate kiss, his tongue teasing at hers, his hands skimming over her body.

But Charlie didn't want to waste time on foreplay. She grabbed the box and pulled out a packet. Ronan moaned softly as she sheathed him, his shaft hard and ready again.

Charlie wasn't prepared for what happened next. As he slowly entered her, a rush of emotion overwhelmed her and she realized that what she was about to share with him would probably change her life.

She'd never forget this man or the pleasure that he'd brought into her world in such a short time. Before he'd arrived, she'd been marking the days, drifting in a routine that was safe but certainly not satisfying.

Ronan slowly buried himself inside her, his lips grazing hers as he bent closer. Charlie held her breath until he could go no further, then let a soft moan escape. As he began to move, she found it difficult to focus on anything but the swirl of sensations coursing through her body.

It had been years since she'd felt this way, like a woman—like a sexy, desirable woman. In truth, maybe she'd never felt this way. And she didn't care how long the affair lasted. A day or a month, it didn't matter. For as long as Ronan wanted her, she would find her way into his bed.

5

RONAN JUMPED OUT of the skiff as Charlie maneuvered it alongside the dock. She grabbed the stern line and quickly knotted it around the cleat, then hurried to the stern to pull that line tight.

They'd been working together for a week and a half and now operated as a finely tuned team. They'd moved from seeding the oyster beds to harvesting, along with three other teams. Their mornings were spent pulling the lantern baskets full of harvested oysters from a spot in the bay.

Those oysters had been sorted and put in the baskets a few days before, then left in free flowing water in order to purge them of grit. After the lantern baskets were delivered to the boathouse for cleaning, packaging and shipping, Charlie and Ronan headed back out to harvest oysters from the bottom, pulling up dredge baskets full of the lumpy shells and sorting them into the lantern baskets.

He hadn't grown tired of the work. In fact, Charlie had been teaching him all about the farm and he was beginning to fall into the easy rhythms and routines. He glanced down at his work partner and smiled.

She was dressed in the typical uniform, rubber boots, chest-high waders, a long-sleeved T-shirt and heavy gloves. Today, she wore a battered Red Sox cap on her head that shaded her eyes from the sun, and her hair, tangled by the salty wind, peeked out from beneath the cap.

She'd never looked more beautiful, he thought to himself. In the past, Ronan had always entered a relationship with a woman knowing full well that it would come to an end within a month. Women had become a commodity and his romantic life had been short on romance and high on turnover.

Was it any wonder that he'd missed out on something like this? Had there been a woman in his past like Charlotte Sibley had? She was bright light, sunshine pouring into the dark corners of his soul.

Ronan jumped back down into the boat and grabbed Charlie, pulling her into a long kiss. "What do you say we get ourselves all dressed up and go out this evening? It's Friday night."

Charlie's eyebrow shot up. "You want to take me on a date?"

"Yeah. There must be somewhere we could go. The movies? Maybe a nice restaurant. I got paid yesterday. And the money is burning a hole in my waders."

"So first, we jump into bed and then we start dating." She grinned. "It didn't work for me the other way around so I guess we could give it a shot."

"All right. I'll make the plans." But before he could

go on, Ronan heard a scream from the wharf above them.

"Charlotte Sibley! Charlotte Sibley, I need youuuuuuu!"

Charlie peeked over Ronan's shoulder and groaned. "Oh, no. Lettie Trowbridge. If you get the lines, I think we should be able to make our escape before she gets down here."

"What does she want?" Ronan asked. He turned around when he heard the clomp of footsteps on the wooden stairs.

"Who knows. She may want an update on our sex life. Or she may want to know whether I read the books she dropped off at my parents' house."

"What kind of books?"

"How To Please Your Man. Catch Your Perfect Guy In Thirty Days. Make Love Like A Porn Star."

"That last one sounds good."

"Charlotte! Hellooo! Charlotte!"

Pasting a smile on her face, Charlie stepped out from behind Ronan and jumped up onto the dock. Lettie was an elderly woman with a shock of white hair that looked like it had been combed with a rake. She wore a blouse with flowers bigger than her head and carried a huge purse that hung from her shoulder.

"Hello," she said, sending him a warm smile. "You must be the Quinn. I've seen you around town, but we haven't officially met." She held out her hand. "Leticia Trowbridge. Sibleyville's official matchmaker." She reached into her purse and pulled out a camera then snapped a quick picture of him.

"Oh, look at that. Rugged. Handsome. The scruffy beard will have all the women swooning." She snapped another picture. "I'd love to get one after you've had a chance to clean up a bit."

"Lettie, is there something I can help you with? You came here looking for me, didn't you?"

The older woman slapped her forehead. "Yes! I did. I am in dire need of your help, Charlotte. As you know, I'm the head of the entertainment and culture committee for the Sibleyville Bicentennial Celebration which will begin two weeks from today. And I'm sure you've heard that we're doing a wonderful theatrical production called 'The Curse of Bridie Quinn.' It's a Romeo and Juliet tale of Edward Sibley and Moira Quinn. Only in this version, they get married."

"You can't change history," Charlie said.

"Of course I can. The whole last part of the play takes place in a dream. At the end, Edward wakes up and stares longingly out to sea. It's very tragic." She paused for a moment as if she'd forgotten her train of thought, then drew another breath. "The reason I've come is that we've lost our Moira. Ruth Ann Robinson tripped over her cat and broke her ankle. There's no way she'll be able to go on. Anyway, everyone in town thought that you'd be an excellent replacement since you were a professional actress at one time."

Ronan grabbed the lunch pail from the skiff and the extra clothes, then jumped onto the dock. "I'm going to head up to the apartment," he said.

"No, no, don't leave," Lettie said. "I understand you know you're way around a hammer and a saw. We could use your help with sets. It would mean a lot to everyone here in town."

"I really don't think I'll have time," he said.

"And I won't either, Lettie."

"But you could memorize everything quickly. You wouldn't have to come to rehearsal until the week after next. I'm sure you'll be able to learn the staging quickly. Please say you'll consider it."

Charlie glanced over at Ronan, shaking her head. "If you don't find anyone else to take the part, then I might consider it. But you should keep looking."

"Lovely," Lettie said. She pulled a sheaf of papers from her bag. "This is the script. Just give it a look. I'd love your input." She turned to Ronan. "And as for you, Mr. Quinn, I'll be keeping my eye on you."

With that, Leticia Trowbridge hurried off the dock, her hair blowing in the late afternoon breeze. Charlie grabbed Ronan's arm and leaned against him.

"I'd love to see you on stage," he murmured.

She gave him a playful slap with the script. "No way."

"I could help you memorize your lines," he said.

"You're going to take me out tonight," she said. "But first, I'm going to go home and take a nice long bath."

"Come on, then." He held her hand as they walked back to the boathouse. The Fed Ex truck was parked outside and the girls from the shipping department were helping to load the boxes of oysters and dry ice. One of the women stopped Charlie to discuss a problem with the previous day's shipments, so Ronan continued on to the boathouse. He stripped out of his boots and waders, then walked up to the apartment in his stocking feet.

As he passed the office, he noticed Charlie's mother, sitting at a desk with a ledger in front of her, her reading glasses perched on the end of her nose. She looked up as he neared and smiled.

"Hello, there," she said.

They hadn't seen each other since his first night in town, over a week ago, and Ronan had to wonder how she felt about her daughter spending her nights in his bed. "Hi," Ronan said.

"You're in early," she said, glancing up at the clock.

"Yeah, we got an early start this morning. And the dredging went really well." He paused. "I wanted to thank you for stocking the kitchen. I really appreciated that."

"I just wanted to make sure you were comfortable. So how do you like oyster farming?"

Ronan smiled. "I like it a lot," he said. "It's so nice to be outdoors and on the water. And I like working with Charlotte." He paused. "I'm sorry that I've been monopolizing her time."

"I'm happy that she has someone to monopolize her time," Penny said. "She's been at loose ends since she came back from New York. And she was spending too much time alone. Of course, we appreciate her help with the farm, but she needs to think about her own happiness."

"You don't think she's happy working on the oyster farm?"

"I think she feels a responsibility to help out the

family. I want her to find her own passion, to chase her own dreams."

She'd been chasing some of her passions with him every night. Since their first night together, they'd found new ways of expressing their desire and each interlude had provided intimate revelations that made his feelings for her grow even deeper.

"We're having Thanksgiving tomorrow night," she said. "We'd like you to come."

"I'd love to," Ronan said.

"Oysters," she said. "I have to take some oysters home for the stuffing. I hope you like oyster stuffing. If you don't, I could—"

"No, no," Ronan said. "Believe me, I'll eat anything that has oysters in it. I think I've eaten them every day since I've been here."

"Hmmm," Penny said. "No wonder my daughter hasn't spent a night at home in all that time." She gave him a shrewd look. "Oh, don't be embarrassed. I happen to think that sex is one of the two things that make life worth living. Food would be the other. I have seven children, proof that Mr. Sibley and I enjoy ourselves in that area." She paused. "Oh, I am embarrassing you. Well, run along. I hope I haven't done too much damage."

Ronan nodded and hurried to the apartment. As he closed the door behind him, he chuckled softly. Talking about sex with Charlie's mother was just about the strangest thing he'd ever done. But then, strange seemed to be almost normal when it came to the Sibley family. Irish curses. Chicken tandoori. Thanksgiving in September. What was next?

CHARLIE CLOSED THE front door of the apartment behind her. As she walked through the living room, she pulled her clothes over her head and tossed them on the floor. "Ronan?"

"I'm in here," he said, his voice coming from the bathroom.

"Mom said she invited you for Thanksgiving tomorrow night?"

"Yeah, we had a nice talk," he said.

Charlie frowned. That very short statement could mean just about anything. "A nice talk?" She opened the bathroom door and froze.

Candles illuminated the interior. They were scattered around the room, the flames flickering in the draft from the air conditioning. Ronan, his hair still damp from a shower, had filled the bathtub and sat on the floor beside it, wearing only his boxers, a glass of wine in his hand.

"What did you do?" she asked.

"You said you wanted a long bath. I made one for you. Hop in before it gets cold."

She squatted down beside him and gave him a kiss. "You're awfully nice to me. You're not angling for a raise are you?"

"I wasn't," he said. "But if this will get me one, I'll crawl in with you."

Charlie stripped off the rest of her clothes, then stepped into the tub. "No, I prefer to take my bath alone. But you can watch." As she slowly sank down into the water, she let out a long breath. "Oh, that's nice."

He handed her the glass of wine, then stretched his

legs out in front of him. "Your mother is very…open-minded."

Charlie nodded. "I know! She's always been that way. We were the first kids in school to know the truth about Santa Claus and the Tooth Fairy. She claimed that she just couldn't perpetuate a lie and she felt guilty deceiving her children past the age of ten."

"We had a nice chat about sex," Ronan said.

"Oh, God, no. Did she tell you the cow story?"

"No," he said.

"Good. I'm not going to tell it to you now, because I'd prefer to save myself the embarrassment. But I'm sure you'll hear it at some point."

"I like your mother," Ronan said. "I'd kind of like to think that my mother might have been a lot like her." He paused. "Since I've been here, there have been some things that I think I remember about her."

"Like what?"

He thought for a long moment. "I remember how much she used to laugh. She and my father always seemed to be sharing a private joke."

"My parents do that all the time. Even at their age, they still can't keep their hands off each other. That was really embarrassing when I was younger. Now, I think it's sweet." Charlie reached out and ran her finger along his arm. "What else do you remember?"

"It's just this vague feeling. Mom always wanted me to make my own choices. I remember one time, I think I was in kindergarten. I had these Superhero pajamas and I wanted to wear them to school. My brothers made all kinds of fun of me, but she backed me up.

She said if I wanted to wear them to school, I could. So I did. And she took a photo of me and her, standing on the porch of our house, on our way to school. I still have that photo."

"She sounds like a wonderful person," Charlie said.

"I think she was. I hope my memories are true. After my parents died, my grandfather never wanted to talk about them. And the older I get, the more I want to know who they were."

"Maybe you should find out," Charlie said. "Have you ever asked your grandfather?"

"No," Ronan said. "Whenever we tried, he'd tear up and get emotional. And he was a really strong man. But he just couldn't talk about it."

Ronan slipped his hand around her nape and drew her into a kiss. His gaze met hers and Charlie saw something there that she'd never seen before. What was it? There were times that he seemed to drift to a distant place and then, suddenly, he'd be back again.

Ronan helped her wash her hair and when she was done, he wrapped a towel around the damp strands. Then he grabbed another towel and gently wiped the water out of her eyes. "I've never been able to talk about this stuff," he said. "I've kept it bottled up inside of me for years. And yet, when I'm with you, it just comes pouring out."

"That's good, isn't it?" she said, her gaze fixed on his.

"Yeah," he murmured. "It is good."

She leaned back and closed her eyes, her fingers still laced through his. "If you want to know more about them, maybe you could find some of their friends. They must have had people that they hung around with. People they talked to."

"I never thought of that," he said.

A long silence grew between them, but Charlie didn't feel compelled to speak. She knew he was thinking about his parents, something he hadn't done very often in the past. Whatever he was working though, she wanted to give him the space to do it.

They shared the glass of wine and when the water in the tub had cooled, she stepped out into a towel he held. He took her hand and walked into the bedroom with her. They curled up on the bed facing each other, talking about the events of the day, discussing the problems she'd encountered and the solutions she'd chosen.

Every day he was learning more about the business and with each day that passed, Charlie was left to wonder if he might just stay in Sibleyville a little longer than he originally planned.

She silently scolded herself. It wouldn't do to plan a future around Ronan. From the beginning they'd been careful to keep their expectations in check. It was enough to enjoy the physical relationship and the emotional attachment, but a real commitment was something entirely different.

"What else did you and my mom talk about?"

"She invited me for Thanksgiving in September tomorrow night."

"Oh, boy, more of my family. I'm not sure that's a good thing."

"I like your family," he said. "They're what I imagine a real family is like. Everyone fits. And you love each other, even though you're all a little crazy. I don't think you realize how lucky you are."

"I know," she said in a soft voice. After hearing Ronan's story, it did make her more appreciative. It was strange how he'd made her look at things so differently. He was making her a better person just by helping her to see her life through clear eyes.

"If you want to do that play, I'll come along and help," Ronan said. "It might be fun."

"I don't know," Charlie replied. "I've kind of left that part of my life behind."

"But if you're good at it, you should do it. And we have some time."

"You mean you want to take time out of our sex life for community theatre."

He chuckled. "Well, if you put it that way, maybe not."

"Let's see if Lettie finds someone else first. If she doesn't, maybe I'll help her out."

He smoothed his hand over her temple, pushing the towel away from her hair. There were moments when she felt so close to him, as if they were connected by a tether strung between their souls. It was a strange feeling because Charlie had always assumed that this was what love was.

But she and Ronan had known each other less than two weeks. Granted, since they'd met, they'd spent every waking, and sleeping, hour together. And they'd even managed to work happily together. Though Ronan had all the confidence in the world, he didn't seem to have an ego, something she'd never seen in the most men she'd known. He was happy to defer to her when it came to work, taking each task she directed in stride.

"Make love to me," she murmured.

Ronan smiled then touched his lips to hers in a gentle kiss. Pulling her against his body, they rolled over until she was on top of him, her legs straddling his hips. He grabbed the towel and pulled it open, revealing her naked body beneath.

As his mouth found her nipple, she wrapped her arms around him, her fingers tangling in his thick hair. Everything she'd ever needed was here in this room. She wanted it to last forever.

But maybe for her, forever would have to come one day at a time.

THE SIBLEY HOUSE was filled with the scents of a Thanksgiving meal. Ronan stood in the foyer and drew a deep breath through his nose, searching for a sense memory of his childhood. But the memories that had bubbled up since he'd arrived in Sibleyville weren't always the kind he could summon at will. They usually snuck up on him, surprising him with their clarity and intensity.

Charlie turned back to him, motioning him forward. "Come on. You've already seen them at their worst."

"The last time I was here, I was just the guy that you'd hired to work the oyster farm. Now, I'm the guy you're sleeping with."

"Are you under the impression that I come from a straight-laced, conservative family? I think they've made it quite clear that Peyton and Penelope Sibley didn't follow the normal rules raising their children."

"Hey, there!" Peyton Sibley appeared from the back of the house, his movement aided by a cane. "It's turkey day. We all love turkey day."

Ronan held out his hand. "Hello, Mr. Sibley."

Peyton grabbed his hand and shook it enthusiastically. "Is my old man here? He's the only Mr. Sibley I've ever known. Now that we know each other, you can call me Peyton."

"Peyton."

"I hear you're doing a bang-up job on the boats. Jake's been telling me that you can haul oysters with the best of them."

"I like the work," Ronan said. "And I'm pretty fond of oysters, too."

Her father laughed. "Well, that will probably change. Most folks would probably enjoy an endless supply of fresh oysters. Me? I'd like a job at Dunkin' Donuts. I could eat donuts all day long."

"No you couldn't." Penny Sibley appeared from behind her husband, stepping up to give her daughter a hug. "Hello, Charlotte. And Ronan, I'm glad you decided to come."

"I wasn't about to miss Thanksgiving in September," he said.

"Well, I thought you might want to avoid me," Penny explained. "After our little sex talk the other day. I fear I might have put you on the spot and I want to—"

"Mother, stop. You don't need to apologize. Just try to remember the difference between your family members and everyone else in the world. You can say whatever you like to us, but the rest of the world doesn't really understand you."

"Mom? Do we have any sulfuric acid?" Garrett came running through the foyer wearing a football helmet and carrying a hatchet. "Hey, Ronan."

"Hey, Garrett."

"Do we, Mom?" he asked, looking up at Penny.

"I don't think so, dear. But you could probably get some down at the drug store. What do you need it for?"

"An experiment," he said. He continued through the foyer and out the front door. "Hey, Isaac, can you drive me to the drug store?"

"Are you sure he should have acid?" Charlie asked.

"I suppose if he knows that he wants sulfuric acid, he's aware of what it does, don't you think?" Penny asked. "Besides, I doubt that Clayton down at the drugstore will sell him acid anyway. But I'd rather let Clayton be the bad guy." She smiled. "I have to get back to my turkey. Find Ronan a drink, dear. He looks uncomfortable."

"Got it!" Abby walked through the foyer, a freshly opened bottle of beer in her hand. "Here you go." She handed the beer to Ronan, then ran up the stairs, singing the refrain from a Lady Gaga song.

Peyton clapped him on the back. "Glad you came back," he said. With that, he wandered into the library and closed the doors behind him.

"Show me your bedroom," Ronan said.

Charlie grabbed his hand and they walked up the stairs to the second floor. But they didn't stop there. She opened a door to another narrower stairway and when they reached the top, he realized they were in the attic. The space had been finished into two bedrooms with a bathroom in between.

"This is where the servants used to live," she said. "Two maids in one room and the cook in the other." Charlie pointed to the door with her name emblazoned on the front with glitter. "This one's mine as you can see."

She opened the door and stepped inside, then waited for him to enter. Ronan wasn't sure what he expected. He'd only ever known Charlie as a grown woman. And when he tried to imagine her as a child, or even as a teenager, the picture became vague and unfocussed.

She sat down on the edge of the bed and watched him as he circled the room, taking in his surroundings. "Are you looking for anything in particular?" she asked.

"No, just checking it all out."

"Why?"

He shrugged. "Curiosity," he said. "Am I the first guy you've ever brought up here?"

"God, no," she said with a laugh. But when he turned to look at her, he saw a blush rise in her cheeks. "Sorry. That came out wrong. No, Danny used to climb up here on occasion. He'd crawl up the trellis to the second floor porch, then climb the drainpipe."

"Tell me about him," Ronan said, searching the photos in her room for a guy who might fit her description.

"I don't have any pictures," she said. "I burned them all after we split up."

"Tell me."

He couldn't help but be curious. After all, she'd spent six years with Danny. She'd thought she was in love. And yet, he was here and Danny was in New York.

"He was handsome and funny and popular," she began. "And he had this confidence that just rubbed off on all the people around him. People just seemed to gravitate toward him. Whenever you saw him, he was always in the middle of a group and everyone was watching him."

"Sounds like the perfect guy," Ronan said, feeling a twinge of envy. In high school, he'd barely attracted the attention of any girls. And those that had been interested were slightly odd, girls who preferred their boyfriends tragic and broken. He was the exact opposite of the typical golden boy.

"He was. But he wasn't the perfect one for me. That's the thing. Most people think that guys like that are generically attractive to every girl. And he was, for a while. But the longer I knew him, the more I came to realize that most of the good stuff about him was on the surface. There wasn't much underneath."

"And that's what you want. A man with depth."

Charlie shrugged. "I guess so."

Ronan grabbed her high school yearbook from the bookshelf and crossed to the bed, flopping down on the mattress behind her. "Let's see. Charlotte Sibley." He flipped though the senior section and found her picture. "You were beautiful even then," he said. "Hell, if we'd gone to high school together, you wouldn't have given me a second look."

"Believe me, I would have looked. In case you haven't noticed, you're pretty hot yourself. You must have had girls following you everywhere."

"Not so much," he said. "Girls thought I was weird."

"No! How?"

"I never talked. I never smiled. I didn't have friends. I mean, I talked to some of the guys in class, but we didn't hang out. I listened to music a lot and usually walked home for lunch just so I wouldn't have to spend time in the cafeteria. And I didn't play any sports." He stopped suddenly, then shook his head. "I don't know how you do it."

"Do what?"

"It's like you flip a switch inside of me and I just start babbling. I can say anything to you. In fact, I can't seem to stop."

Charlie sighed, then rested back across his chest, pulling the yearbook out of his hands. She worked at the buttons of his shirt, then pressed a kiss to the center of his chest. "I think that's a very good thing."

"What are you starting," he said, rebuttoning his shirt.

"I'm just kissing you," she said.

"Not here. Not in your parents' house."

Charlie laughed at him. "My parents own the apartment at the boathouse, so technically, that's their place, too."

"What if someone walks in?"

She jumped off the bed and walked to the door, then pulled it closed and locked it. "Better?"

"No. Now if someone tries to open the door, they're going to know what we're doing in here."

"Don't be such a prude." She grabbed his hand and placed it on her breast and Ronan gave her an impatient glare. "There is something kind of exciting about doing it here."

He crawled off the bed, shaking his head. She was teasing him and he wasn't going to let her get away with it. "No way. Besides, I'd only be second best in that bed, after your friend, Danny."

"Oh, now I understand. You're jealous." She jumped off the bed and crossed the room, slipping her arms around his waist. "There's nothing to be jealous of."

"Yes, there is," Ronan murmured. He cupped her face in his palm and kissed her. "He had you for six years. He had a life with you. He saw you every day and every night for months on end."

"Maybe it's the quality instead of the quantity," she said.

"What does that mean?"

"I had all those days and nights with him. But all of them put together didn't even come close to those that we've had. Danny and I were kids. We had no idea what passion really was."

"And now you do?" he asked.

Charlie nodded. "I think maybe I finally have it figured out." She cocked her head toward the bed. "I can show you if you want."

"You can try. But you're going to have to do it with your clothes on. And with my clothes on. Using only your lips."

"Oh, a challenge." She grabbed his hand and dragged him over to the bed, then gave him a gentle shove. He fell backwards onto the mattress. Charlie laid down on top of him, pinning his hands over his head.

"Happy Thanksgiving," she murmured.

"You are crazy," he said just before she captured his mouth in a playful kiss.

"And you're starting to like crazy," she said. "Admit it."

He groaned as she kissed him again. In truth, he needed her, crazy or not. He'd come to appreciate her quirky personality and irresistible smile. And in the end, he'd do anything to keep her in his life.

6

"IF YOU BEND this just a little bit, it should be okay."

Charlie stood over the broken dredge basket and shook her head. "No, no, you can't bend that."

"Sure you can," Ronan replied.

"It will break and then the whole basket will be useless."

"No, it's not that kind of steel."

"I know what my dredge baskets are made of," she said.

"And I know the characteristics of metal. I do have an engineering degree."

She looked up, surprised by his admission. "You do?"

He nodded. "Yeah. And that little piece of metal right there will bend. Once it does, the basket will work."

"You never told me you went to college."

Ronan grabbed the basket out of the bottom of the skiff and hefted it up on the deck, then jumped out of the boat. "It never came up."

"Yes, it did. We talked about how I skipped college

for New York and how you went to work for your grandfather's business."

"Well, I went to college. Not away to college. I lived at home and took a lot of night classes." He braced his hand on his waist and stared down at her. "Is this a problem? Are we having a fight?"

"No," Charlie said. "I—I'm just trying to explain that I—" She cursed softly. "Never mind. Just take the basket up to the shop."

He held out his hand to her. "Come on."

She climbed out of the skiff and the moment both feet were on the dock, he pulled her into an embrace. "Kiss me," he said.

She dropped a quick kiss on his lips.

"You can do better than that," Ronan said.

Frustrated, Charlie decided to make her point in the only way she knew how. She slipped her hand around his neck and pulled him into the most passionate kiss she could manage. She seduced him with her tongue and her lips, refusing to retreat until she knew he couldn't take anymore. "Better?" she asked as she stepped back.

He laughed softly. "Ah, yeah." He hugged her again. "Good thing I'm wearing waders."

He took her hand and they walked up to the boathouse. Charlie was surprised to see her youngest brother, Garrett, sitting on the step for the front door. He glanced up as they approached, then jumped to his feet.

"Hey, Ronan. I brought my video games over. I thought maybe you might want to play a little."

Ronan glanced over at Charlie and she smiled. After dinner Saturday evening, Ronan and Garrett had teamed up against Isaac and Ethan in a video game battle. Isaac and Ethan had always been very close, with Garrett usually the odd brother out. But once he'd claimed Ronan for his side, Garrett seemed to think that the scales were back in balance.

"Is there a system in the apartment?"

"In my dad's office," Garrett said. "He put it there for when we were younger and we'd come to the boathouse after school. But we can hook it up in the apartment."

"Well, all right. I guess I'm up for some fun before dinner. If that's all right with Charlie."

Garrett turned to his older sister, a hopeful look on his face. "Is it all right?"

"Sure," she said. "Maybe you can stay and have pizza with us. How does that sound?"

Garrett grinned. "That would be cool."

Ronan opened the door to the boathouse and ushered Charlie and her brother inside. "Why don't you get the system set up," Ronan suggested, "while I get cleaned up. I'll meet you upstairs in a few minutes."

Garrett raced to the door for the stairway and they both listened as he ran up the stairs. "I guess our plans have been made for us," he murmured, grabbing her hand and weaving his fingers through hers.

Charlie couldn't help but feel a flood of affection for him. He'd been so sweet to Garrett at dinner and it was clear that he understood the way her brother was feeling—like an outsider. "Thank you," she said. "You didn't have to do that."

"No, I wanted to. Hey, if it's a choice between video

games and hot sex with the most beautiful girl in Sibleyville, I'm afraid I have to go with the video games."

Charlie gasped and gave him a playful slap. "So that's how it is?"

"No. Garrett's a good kid. And I like to play video games. It's no fun to play them alone. Believe me, I did that enough as a kid."

Charlie gave him a hug. "You're a nice guy, Ronan Quinn."

He gave her a quick kiss. "Come on. Let's go get cleaned up and then maybe Garrett will let you play with us."

"No, I think I'll leave you two to have your fun."

They both stripped out of their waders and boots and put them on the rack near the door, then walked upstairs. Ronan took a quick shower, then joined Garrett in setting up the X-box on the apartment television.

Charlie called for the pizza and left enough cash on the counter to pay for it, then retired to the bathroom. She'd grabbed the script for Lettie's play, then filled the tub with warm water, adding a measure of her favorite lavender bath salts at the end.

She tossed her work clothes on a pile and stepped into the tub, then sank down beneath the surface until the water covered her body completely. A tiny moan slipped from her lips and she closed her eyes.

Over the past few weeks, she and Ronan had fallen into an easy daily routine, their days spent on the water working and their nights in his bed, discovering the pleasure between them. The more time she spent with

Ronan, the more she realized that a life with him could be something very good.

The notion had snuck up on her. She didn't want to think of Ronan as a potential husband. Thoughts like that frightened her. But she could imagine him staying with her, for another month or another year, or even longer.

She grabbed a washcloth from the rack next to the tub and dampened it, then put it over her face, the scent of lavender filling her head. Her thoughts drifted to the man in her life and she couldn't help but smile at herself. He was her man, at least temporarily. He made it clear to her every day in a million ways that they were a couple.

Charlie had always been so clear about the direction of her life. She'd seen her dreams and gone after them. The move to New York when she was eighteen had been bold and determined. But for some reason, she couldn't do the same with Ronan. Even though her feelings for him had grown deeper with each day, even though she couldn't imagine the moment that he'd walk out of her life, she wasn't prepared to make him her dream.

With a soft sigh, she reached out for the script that she'd dropped on the floor beside the tub. She held it out in front of her and began to read, but it only took a few pages to know that Lettie's theatrical talents lay somewhere other than play writing.

"The Curse of Bridie Quinn" was an overwrought melodrama that had no resemblance to Romeo and Juliet at all. Bridie was a mix of the Wicked Witch of the West and Cruella DeVille. Edward was a typical brooding anti-hero in the mold of Heathcliff. And Moira was a reasonable copy of Blanche DuBois from "Streetcar."

Some of the dialogue was laughable and the rest made her cringe. But for an amateur show, it would do what it was supposed to do, entertain. She made a mental note to call Lettie and tell her that she was going to be out of town on the night of the play so she'd be unable to step in, no matter what the circumstances.

She dropped the play on the floor. Her life as an actress seemed a long way away right now. Though she'd loved every minute of it, she could barely remember the woman she had been a year ago. So much had changed over that time. So much had changed since Ronan had arrived.

Charlie closed her eyes and let her body relax into the scented water. Her thoughts continued to drift, touching on images of Ronan, in her bed, his naked body stretched out beside her. A delicious warmth seeped through her body and for a moment, she felt herself caught up in the dream.

A soft knock sounded on the door and Charlie opened her eyes. A few seconds later, Ronan peeked in. "Pizza's here," he said.

"I'll be out in a few seconds," she said.

"You do know that I'd rather be in here with you, don't you?"

She smiled. "Yes. But we can pick up on that later."

He closed the door behind him and Charlie sighed. There were moments that she didn't want to believe how wonderful her life had become for fear that it would all change tomorrow. How much longer could she deny her feelings for him? No matter how she tried to rationalize their relationship, she knew one thing for certain. She was falling in love with Ronan Quinn.

RONAN RUBBED THE sleep out of his eyes. The early morning light had turned the eastern sky a dusky blue and the area around the wharf was beginning to come alive with everyday activity. He'd left Charlie in bed to get a few more minutes of sleep while he went out to fetch bearclaws for their breakfast.

In Seattle, he'd always eaten a healthy breakfast. But he worked so hard out on the oyster beds that a bearclaw or two was burned off by nine in the morning. He pushed open the front door to the bakery and nodded at the patrons who had become familiar to him over the past three weeks.

The older woman behind the counter smiled at him as he grabbed a numbered ticket from the roll. Ronan walked over to one of the small tables and picked up a discarded copy of the Boston Globe, distractedly scanning the front page.

"I thought I might see you here."

Ronan slowly lowered the paper to find the smiling face of Leticia Trowbridge standing on the other side. Though he'd only had a couple of encounters with her, he knew that she'd come looking for him for a reason. Was she about to enlist him in convincing Charlie to appear in her play? Or was there something else on her mind?

"Hello," Ronan said. "How are you?"

"I'm wonderful. Well, not exactly wonderful. My

play is a disaster of monumental proportions. I can't seem to find the talent I need to really make the roles sing with authenticity. Have you ever aspired to the stage, Mr. Quinn?"

"No, no, no," Ronan said. "I'm not one who enjoys the spotlight."

"Well, the spotlight would certainly enjoy you," she said. "Come and sit down. I have a very serious matter to discuss with you."

"I—I really have to go. Time to get to work."

Lettie pointed to the ticket. "But you haven't been called yet. I only need a few minutes. I promise."

"All right," Ronan said. He nodded toward one of the tables and they sat down across from each other. "What can I do for you?"

"You can marry Charlotte Sibley."

Her words caught him by surprise and his first reaction was to laugh uneasily. But when he did, everyone in the shop turned around to look. "Are you kidding?" he whispered.

"Oh, no. Let me be as direct as possible. The village of Sibleyville pays me a yearly salary to act as matchmaker for the single residents who desire my help. But with your arrival in town, I have the ability to make the very last match this town will ever need. I'm here to ask you how much it would take for you to marry Charlotte."

"Take?" He frowned. "Are you talking about money?"

"Yes. Or some other type of compensation if you

prefer. A car? Property? I'm not sure what you might want."

Ronan shook his head. "You're going to pay me to marry Charlotte?"

"Is there any other way we might convince you to marry her?"

"No," Ronan said. "I—I mean, I'm not going to marry her for money. Not that I don't want to marry her, but—but—" He cursed beneath his breath. "This is really a ridiculous conversation."

"If you marry her, the Sibley and Quinn families will finally be united. The curse will be broken and perhaps more of our young people will choose to fall in love and stay in Sibleyville."

Ronan glanced around at the patrons in the shop. They'd all gone back to their business and no one seemed interested in the conversation going on at Ronan's table. But he had no doubt every ear was trained on their conversation. "Have you talked to Charlie about this?"

"Of course I have."

"What did she say?"

"That she would consider it."

The answer shocked Ronan. Though Charlie wasn't afraid to show her affection for him, they'd never really discussed the future. Actually, she seemed to purposely avoid any mention of what might come of their relationship at the end of six weeks. Had she really considered marriage a possibility for them?

As Lettie chattered on, Ronan couldn't help but wonder what was really going on in Charlie's head. There were moments during their workdays when he'd watch her and know, deep inside his soul, that he'd never be able to let her go. But those thoughts hadn't yet transformed into a real plan for his life. It seemed that all the planning was being done by Lettie.

The woman behind the counter called Ronan's number and he jumped up from the table, grateful for the excuse to end the conversation. "It was really a pleasure," he said. "Have a nice day."

He hurried to the counter and ordered three bearclaws, laying the money out in front of him. The moment the clerk handed him the bag, he hurried out of the bakery.

As he walked back to the apartment, he decided that maybe it was time to talk about the future. He'd been in Sibleyville for exactly three weeks now. He knew the last three weeks would fly by faster than the first three. Nothing he could do would slow them down. So why not just stay? Why not forget the six-week deadline and stay until *he* wanted to leave?

He had a job that he could keep. He was learning more and more every day about the operation of the oyster farm. He'd already found a way to make himself indispensable—at least to Charlie. But he would have to work out this living situation.

Charlie had refused to take rent out of his paycheck and he couldn't continue living in the apartment for free. If he was going to set up a life in Sibleyville, then he'd have to close out his life in Seattle.

When he got back to the apartment, he found Charlie still sleeping soundly. They'd had a lot of late nights, spent in the pursuit of pleasure, and maybe the lack of sleep was beginning to catch up with her. He walked out to the kitchen and poured a cup of coffee into a mug, then carried it into the bedroom.

"Are you trying to wake me up?" she murmured, her eyes still closed.

"I thought you were still sleeping."

"No, I heard you come in." She sat up and brushed the hair from her eyes, then took the mug of coffee from his hand. "Thanks." She took a careful sip and then sighed. "I could use another three or four hours of sleep."

"Why don't you stay in bed? I can find my way to work on my own. And I'll just work on Jake's skiff today. You can have the whole day to yourself."

"No," she said. "I'll be fine once I have a few cups of coffee. We've got a lot to do today. And the bicentennial celebration starts next week. I want to harvest more this week and then give everyone Friday off since they have to work our food booth for a shift over the weekend."

He tucked an errant strand of hair behind her ear. "All right. But instead of engaging in other activities tonight we're going to go to bed and sleep."

She stretched out across his lap, her head resting on his thigh. "We keep saying we should do that, but we never do. Why is that?"

Ronan smoothed his hand over her hair. "Because I can't keep my hands off you. Maybe I should seek out professional help."

"What? Go to a hooker? We don't have any of those in Sibleyville."

"No! Go to a shrink. Someone who can help me stifle my desires."

"We don't have any shrinks in Sibleyville either. We're New Englanders. When we have a problem we just suck it up and get on with our lives. Besides, I don't want you to get rid of your desires. I've grown rather fond of them." She sat up and kissed him, nuzzling at his lips until he returned the favor. And when he was lost in the kiss, she gently pulled him back into bed.

Ronan groaned softly as his hands ran freely over her naked body. He'd grown so accustomed to touching her whenever it pleased him. "If you start this now, we're really going to be late for work."

"I'm the boss," she said.

He chuckled. "Yes, you are."

"And as the boss, I order you to remove your clothes and come back to bed."

It wasn't a difficult decision to make. Ronan followed his boss's request and stripped out of his clothes, then seduced her slowly and deliberately, taking the time to tease her until she begged for release.

And when she did, Ronan buried himself deep inside her, her body convulsing around his until he could no longer maintain his control. They were more together than either one of them could hope to be alone. And with every moment of exquisite pleasure that they shared, Ronan came closer to the conclusion that he couldn't live without her.

"Tonight, we'll crawl into bed early and just sleep," he whispered. "I promise. No messing around."

She kissed him again. "All right." Charlie drew a

deep breath and sat up, then retrieved the coffee mug from the bedside table.

"And there are some things I want to talk to you about," Ronan added.

She frowned. "That sounds serious."

"It is."

"Maybe we should talk now," she suggested.

"It'll wait." He hadn't quite decided how to begin the conversation about their future. But with everyone in town hellbent on putting them together, it was time for the two of them to decide what it was that *they* wanted.

THEY WALKED TOGETHER up to the boathouse, Ronan's arm thrown around her shoulder. It was a perfect relationship, she mused as she laughed at a silly joke Ronan had told. They got along as if they'd known each other for three decades rather than three weeks. And though they spent almost twenty-four hours a day together, it hadn't caused any problems in their relationship. They seemed perfectly suited to each other, a match that seemed almost too good to be true.

"Charlie!"

She looked up to find Michelle, her cousin, standing on the wharf above them. Michelle handled the shipping for Mistry Bay Oyster Farm. She worked afternoons, from one to five, packing oysters into dry ice and boxing them up to ship overnight.

"Hey!" Charlie called. "What's up?"

"We've got a huge problem."

"Hang on," she said. "I'll be up in a second."

She and Ronan climbed the stairs and found Michelle

waiting for them, a clipboard clutched in her hands, a worried look on her face.

"I'm gonna go clean up," Ronan said. "I'll see you upstairs."

Charlie and Michelle watched him walk the short distance to the boathouse and when he disappeared inside, Michelle sighed dramatically. "What a hunk," she muttered. She turned back to Charlie. "Are you going to marry him?"

"No!" Charlie said. "Have you been listening to Lettie?"

"Your mother," she said. "My mother. My aunt. Three of my cousins. The whole town is talking." She leaned close to Charlie. "I heard that Lettie approached your Ronan this morning at the bakery and offered him money!"

"For what?" Charlie asked.

"To marry you. I guess the village board authorized an emergency expenditure. And some of the folks have started a fund at the bank. They want to find a way to keep him here in town."

"Oh, God," Charlie murmured. "This has gotten completely out of hand." She reached out and patted Michelle's arm. "Thanks for telling me. If there's anything else, just—"

"That's not the problem," Michelle said.

"It's not?"

"No. We screwed up the Bellingham order," she said, wincing. "I don't know how it happened, but we put the wrong address on the package and it's going to one of our restaurants in New York instead of Boston. We tried to catch it, but once it's in the system, we can't." She sighed. "And this is his first order so we have a lot riding on it. His soft opening is tomorrow night."

"All right," she said. "Pack up another order. In fact, double the number and I'll take them down this evening. It's only a three-hour drive. I'll drop them at the restaurant and come right back."

"I can do that, Charlotte," Michelle said. "It's my fault. I didn't double check the address after we put it in the system."

Charlie shook her head. "No, I really need to get out of town for awhile." Her thoughts wandered back to earlier that morning. Ronan had come back from the bakery and mentioned he had some things he wanted to discuss that evening. After Michelle's revelation, Charlie knew exactly what would be on the agenda.

This kind of pressure wasn't fair to him. He'd come to town hoping to find a job and a place to live for six weeks. He hadn't bargained for an Irish curse, a misguided marriage proposal and two-thousand anxious citizens watching his every move.

"Leave the oysters on the work table and I'll grab them," Charlie said.

"Thanks," Michelle replied. "And it won't happen again, I promise."

"Hey, it's no big deal. At least we have a chance to fix it."

When she got inside the boathouse, she tossed off her waders and boots and ran up the stairs. As she walked inside, she stripped off her work clothes and tossed them into an empty laundry basket, then walked naked to the bathroom.

The room was filled with steam and she opened the door to the shower stall and stepped inside, smoothing her hand over Ronan's back.

"Hey, there," he said, glancing over his shoulder in surprise.

"Switch."

He grabbed her waist and turned them both, putting her beneath the warm spray. Charlie let the water sluice through her hair, then grabbed the shampoo.

"Let me do that," he said, taking the bottle from her.

She turned and tipped her head back. Ronan poured a bit of shampoo onto her head and slowly worked it through her wet hair. She closed her eyes and let his massaging fingers do their work. He always knew exactly how to touch her, how to make her feel excited or relaxed, desperate or determined. He read her moods like he owned the manual.

"You know, taking a shower together is not going to help us avoid sex tonight."

"Oh, right," Charlie said. "Well, forget that."

"I thought you wanted to get some sleep."

"We can't. We're driving to Boston as soon as we get out of the shower."

"Boston?"

Charlie finished rinsing her hair and opened her eyes, looking up into this handsome face. "There was a mistake in the delivery address for the Bellingham order. Remember Chef Joel? His restaurant opens tomorrow and he needs oysters. Right now his oysters are on their way to some restaurant in New York City. So we're taking him his order."

"Yeah? How far is it?"

"Three hours. I was thinking maybe we could have dinner there. Spend the night. Get a hotel. I need a day away from this town."

"You need a day to relax."

"We'll make it up day after tomorrow."

He cupped her face in his hands and gave her a long, deep kiss. "I'm going to get out of this shower before I take advantage of you."

"Wear something nice," she said. "We may go to an expensive restaurant."

"I'll do that," Ronan said.

He stepped out of the shower, leaving Charlie to finish on her own. She felt a surge of excitement at the thought of getting out of town. Though she enjoyed the routine that she and Ronan had fallen into, it was time to shake things up. If he thought he knew her, then this was a good opportunity for her to prove that there were still some surprises between them.

She finished her shower, then stepped out, wrapping a towel around her body. She wiped the steam off the mirror and looked at her reflection. A summer spent in the sun had given her a golden tan along with a light dusting of freckles across her nose. Charlie raked her fingers through her damp hair, pulling it away from her face, then reached for her make-up case.

She hadn't worn make-up in months. She'd left all the girly beauty routines behind in New York. But it was time to show Ronan that she wasn't just the plain old tomboy he thought she was. She could be glamorous and exotic and seductive if she wanted to.

After she finished with her make-up, she dried and curled her hair, fashioning it into a rumpled finger-curled style that had been her customary look as an actress. She looked…sexy.

She peeked out of the bathroom door. The bedroom was empty and Ronan's duffel was sitting on the end of the bed, packed. Charlie kept a few nice dresses at the apartment for business meetings. She found her favorite flowered sundress and slipped into it, the low cut back making it impossible to wear a bra. After pulling on a pair of lacy panties, she slipped her feet into her favorite sandals, then looked at herself in the mirror.

"All right," she murmured. "Time to shake things up."

"Hey, should I load the oysters into—" Ronan stopped dead the moment he saw her standing in the middle of the bedroom. He frowned and then a slow smile broke over his face. "Wow. Holy…wow. You look incredible."

His reaction was exactly what she needed. She felt beautiful and sexy and to have him react the way he did made her spirits soar. Everyone in town might have a vested interest in their relationship, but it really was all about this—the current of attraction that crackled between them.

"I just thought I'd dress up a little."

"You look so beautiful. Not that you don't look beautiful every other day. Because you do. You always look beautiful. But this is…different."

She smiled. "Thank you. Let me just put a few things in a bag and we'll be ready to go. We'll take the SUV. If you want, you can grab the boxes of oysters from the table downstairs and put them in the truck. I'll be down in a few minutes."

Ronan grabbed his duffel and slipped the strap over his shoulder. Then he crossed the room and pulled her into a lingering kiss. "I'm really looking forward to this," he said.

"You should be," Charlie said. "You might just get lucky tonight."

"With you?"

"Who else?"

"Are you wearing underwear?"

"Bottoms. No top."

He groaned. "All right. Well, I really didn't need to know that. Maybe you should put underwear on. It's going to be really distracting for me."

"I can't," she said. "Not with this dress. Do you want me to change?"

"Nope. I'm just gonna go put the oysters in the car. I'll meet you downstairs."

Charlie giggled softly as he hurried out of the room. No matter how she was dressed or how raggedy she looked, Ronan always made her feel like the most beautiful woman on the planet.

After she'd returned from New York, she hadn't really known what her life would be. She'd been waiting, wondering if anything—or anyone—might come along to change the course of her existence. And now that Ronan had, she felt as if her future might just lie with him. She had no idea where that might be or what they'd do, but since the moment she'd met him, she hadn't been able to picture her life without Ronan Quinn in it.

"Maybe it's time to talk about the future," she murmured as she grabbed a bag from the floor of the closet. A shiver of indecision skittered through her and she wondered if it might be too soon. But she wanted to call the terms, not leave it to Lettie and her town council. She needed to know how Ronan felt before all the busybodies started to weigh in on their prospects.

It would be tempting to stay in Boston a little longer. But one night would have to be enough. When they returned tomorrow, she'd have a better idea of where she stood with Ronan. And that was all she needed for now.

7

IT WAS A beautiful September night in Boston and after Ronan and Charlie had delivered the oysters to Chef Joel's new restaurant, he'd invited them to stay for dinner. At a small table in a quiet corner of the upscale bistro, they dined on diver scallops, red prawns and tiramisu for dessert.

Stuffed and sleepy, they decided to take a walk before looking for a hotel for the night. They hadn't had a lot of time to just relax and enjoy each other's company in public back in Sibeyville, spending most of their time alone at the apartment. For some odd reason, Ronan suddenly felt a little bit nervous away from his comfort zone.

Their respective roles in Sibleyville had been carefully outlined from the moment they met, but now, without the structure of a workday or the passion of a night in bed, he wasn't quite sure what was expected of him.

He wanted to talk to her about his encounter with Lettie in the bakery shop. He wanted to know how she felt about the plans they were making for her. But if he and Charlie had done one thing in their short time together, and done it well, they'd avoided talking about their relationship. He'd never been one to enjoy dissecting the dynamics between himself and a woman, but then, he'd never been particularly interested in what women had to say about him.

But with Charlie he felt differently. He wanted to know exactly where he stood with her. Was she falling for him as hard as he'd fallen for her? Did she think about a future together? Or was she simply enjoying herself until he got back on the bus and drove out of her life?

"You've been quiet," Charlie said. "Are you all right?"

Ronan nodded. He drew her hand up to his lips and kissed the soft skin on the inside of her wrist. "I'm great. It's nice to get away. I've always wanted to visit Boston. I think I have some distant cousins here. At least that's what my grandfather tells us."

"Maybe you *are* related to Bridie Quinn," she said. "Bridie came from Boston, too."

Another long silence grew between them. They usually had so much to talk about. Ronan searched for a subject but all that came to mind were the questions he had about the future. "I—I suppose Sibleyville must seem really small to you after living in New York."

She nodded, then stopped dead and turned to him, her gaze intent. "I know about what happened this morning at the bakery and I'm really sorry."

"How did you—"

"It's a small town, Ronan. Everyone knows everything about everybody. You certainly didn't deserve that. And I want you to know that what's going on with Lettie and the rest of the town has nothing to do with me."

"Of course I know that." He slipped his arms around her waist and pulled her against his body. "So you think I should refuse all that money? I was kind of thinking that I could use a little extra cash."

Her serious expression faded and she laughed. "Believe me, I'm the last person any man would want to marry."

He frowned. Did she actually believe what she was saying? In his mind, she was quickly becoming his first pick for a happily-ever-after. "And why is that?"

"I'm kind of bossy."

"Yes, you are."

"And I like to do what I like to do."

"Yes, I've noticed that, too. But those aren't really deal breakers. I kind of like you just the way you are."

"Kind of?"

He nodded.

Charlie hugged him tight. "You are the only man who has ever said that to me."

"Correct me if I'm wrong, but there's only been one other man in your life. And he was an idiot who let you go."

She took his hand and they continued their walk. "Yes, that is true."

Ronan reached out and brushed a strand of wind-blown hair from her eyes, then tucked it behind her ear. "So, do you think you need to go out there and try out a few more guys, just to be sure that you have the right one? Or is two enough?"

The moment he said the words, he knew they hadn't come out right. He'd meant to tease her, but his question sounded more like an upside down proposal. Hell, maybe it was. Maybe, deep down, he wanted to be the last man she ever kissed…or touched…or crawled into bed with.

"I'm not sure," she murmured.

Her answer took him by surprise. Yes, the question was clumsily worded. But her reply was quite clear. "So you do have plans to move on to someone else?"

"I don't have any plans," she snapped. "I haven't made plans since I came back from New York."

He shook his head. "Go ahead, say it, Charlie. I'm just the guy you're sleeping with for six weeks."

"No!" she cried. "That's not it."

"Then how is it? Tell me. Because I'd kinda like to know where I stand with you."

She hurried on ahead. "I really don't want to talk about this right now. Can we just find the SUV and go?"

"I thought we were going to stay for the night?"

"No. No, I just want to get home. Everything feels so different here. I don't like it."

She looked so upset that Ronan wasn't sure what to do. He'd always known Charlie to be cool and in control, but she seemed like she was dancing on the edge of a meltdown. Hell, he never knew what to do in situations like this. He could barely identify his own emotions, much less read those of the feminine variety.

Should he kiss her? Should he ask her what's wrong?

Or should he just find her a tissue and let her cry it out? She wanted to go home, so he'd work on that first. Hopefully, the rest would solve itself along the way.

After a short search for the SUV, they found it parked near Joel Bellingham's new restaurant. Charlie opened the locks with her keyfob, but then Ronan took the keys from her fingers and helped her into the passenger side. "I'll drive," he murmured.

"Fine," she said.

He settled himself behind the wheel and started the engine, then pulled out into traffic. He didn't really know where he was going, but Ronan wasn't about to ask for help. The atmosphere was so tense he was afraid that whatever was keeping her silent would suddenly snap.

It took a bit of driving around before he found a sign for the interstate, but a few minutes later they were pulling onto I-93 heading out of the city.

"I thought I'd have everything figured out by now," she said. "I thought I knew what my life was supposed to be and when that didn't work out, there wasn't anything else I really wanted. I guess I've just been waiting around for something to drop out of the sky at my feet." She turned to face him. "And then you did. And I wanted you."

Ronan reached out and slid his fingers through the hair at her nape. "There's nothing wrong with that, is there?"

"Not on the surface. But I can't figure out if I want you because I have nothing else or if I want you because you're supposed to be in my life." She cursed softly.

"And it doesn't help that the sex is so good, because that really confuses things."

"You'd rather we had bad sex?"

"No. But it would certainly make sorting out my feelings a lot easier."

"What do you want, Charlie?"

"I don't have a clue. I'm twenty-five years old. People are supposed to have it all figured out by now."

"I'm twenty-six and I'm still trying to figure it out," Ronan said. "But I think I'm getting closer."

Charlie studied him for a long moment. "What does that mean?"

Ronan wasn't sure how much he ought to say. He and Charlie had always been pretty honest with each other. And maybe it was time to admit his feelings for her. "I like Sibleyville. I like working on the farm with you. And I really like you. A lot."

"I—I really like you, too." She let out a long sigh. "And that's enough, right? We don't need to say anymore than that."

She seemed to be so happy with the decision that Ronan didn't have the heart to push Charlie any further. "What are we going to do about Lettie?"

"Ignore her?" Charlie suggested. "I know, that won't work. But she honestly believes that marrying the two of us off will break the curse. She's not going to let up until we're walking down the aisle or we both leave town."

Ronan ran his hand down her arm and tangled his fingers in hers. "Do you think she's right? Do you think the curse could be broken if we got married?"

"My family has always said that the curse was utter

nonsense. When Danny and I ran off to New York, everyone thought that it was finally broken. Two people from Sibleyville were in love and would finally end up together. Only when it didn't work out, everyone was disappointed. I feel badly because it's my ancestors' fault that there was a curse in the first place. No one in Sibleyville falls in love with each other because they believe in the curse. And they believe in the curse because no one in Sibleyville falls in love with each other."

"What do they call that?"

"Crazy," she muttered.

"No, a self-fulfilling prophecy."

"Exactly," Charlie said. "It happens because they believe it's going to happen. So why do I have to be a part of it all?"

"I think you should stop worrying about everyone else," Ronan said.

"That's easier said than done."

He took her hand and pressed it to his lips. "I promise I'll do my best to help."

Ronan wasn't sure what he could do for her, especially against an entire town who wanted to marry her off to a guy she'd just met three weeks ago. Considering that guy was him, he ought to be a bit more concerned. But the thought of marrying Charlie, of spending the rest of their lives together, didn't frighten him at all. In fact, it intrigued him.

Was this how it was all supposed to happen? Was this how he'd realize he was in love? His mind told him that falling in love in three weeks was impossible. But there had been something between them from the very start, a powerful, undeniable attraction. At first, he'd thought it was just sexual. But now, he knew it was more.

Ronan looked at the next exit coming up and noticed the name of a nice hotel chain. He didn't want to spend another three hours waiting to touch her and kiss her. He wanted Charlie in his arms and in his bed right now.

He pulled over to the off ramp and she glanced at him. "Where are we going?"

"To get a room," he said.

"I thought we were going back home."

Ronan shook his head. "Nope. Home is three hours away and I need to take care of a few things right now."

Once they parked at the hotel, it took him exactly fourteen minutes to register and get their key. They rode up the elevator in silence. But when Ronan opened the door to the room, need took over. Desperate, overwhelming, undeniable need.

Ronan pulled her body against his and captured her mouth in a fierce, possessive kiss. She responded immediately, her fingers fumbling with the zipper of his khakis. When she freed him, she quickly smoothed the latex over his hard shaft.

Grabbing her backside, he picked her up and wrapped her legs around his waist. Everything had moved so fast and then, suddenly, slowed again. The delicious sensation of burying himself deep inside of her stole the breath from his body and Ronan paused, his lips pressed into the curve of her neck.

As he drew on his self-control, Ronan had only one thought in his mind. This woman had stolen his heart and his soul. And he really didn't care.

CHARLIE GOT THE phone call from Lettie at six p.m., while she and Ronan were getting ready to make some dinner for themselves. When she saw Lettie's name on her caller I.D., she put the phone down, refusing to answer. But then a minute later, it rang again. Lettie was nothing if not tenacious.

"Hello, Lettie."

"Charlotte? I'm sorry to be calling you at such a late date. I know you're not anxious about resuming your career as an actress, but I've run out of choices. I need you to fill in. Opening night is just four days away."

"I thought you were going to try to get someone else," Charlie said.

"I'd convinced Emma Woburn to do it. But once we got to the stage kiss, she just couldn't. She has a terrible fear of germs, and she simply refused."

"Cut the kiss, then," Charlie said. "That's easy enough to do."

"No, the kiss is the climax of the entire play. I couldn't possibly do it. Besides, Emma was just horrid. She couldn't act her way out of a paper bag, even if you gave her a roadmap and a pair of scissors."

Charlie glanced over the counter to find Ronan watching her closely. "Maybe you should make a deal with her," he whispered.

She covered the phone. "What kind of deal?"

"If you do her play, she lays off the marriage talk."

Charlie grinned at the suggestion. "Lettie, I'll do it. Under one condition. You forget all about your plans to marry me off to Ronan Quinn."

The demand was met with twenty seconds of silence. "Lettie, are you still there?"

"All right," she finally said. "Fine. What's the point anyway? If I want to live with my sister, she can move back to Sibleyville."

"It's a deal," she said. "When do you need me?"

"Now," Lettie replied. "And bring your tap shoes."

"There's tap dancing?"

"Not yet. But I may add some if the mood strikes me."

Charlie switched off the phone and looked up at Ronan. He was having a hard time holding back his laughter. "Stop," she warned. "If you laugh at me, I will find a way to get you up on the stage with me."

He held out his hands in mock surrender. "No, no. Not me."

She pointed at him, her eyes narrowed. "Then stop it."

"I'm just looking forward to seeing tap dancing in a play about a nineteenth century Irish witch. That could be very interesting."

She circled the counter and stood in front of Ronan who was sitting on a kitchen stool. "You're going to come with me."

"Is that really necessary?"

"Yes. You can help me with my lines. The only thing that will make this remotely tolerable is you. And I know exactly what's going to happen the minute I set foot in that theater. Everyone is going to be pushing Lettie's plan—except Lettie."

"All right," he said. He grabbed the car keys from the

counter, then pulled a bottle of water from the fridge. "What else do you need? Should I go out and get you an entourage? Maybe a few celebrity photographers? How about a red carpet?"

She walked over to him and grabbed the front of his shirt, twisting it in her fingers. "Listen, Ronan Quinn. If you don't stop teasing me about this I will never kiss you again. Ever."

"You couldn't stop kissing me if you tried." He pulled her into his arms and bent close, but Charlie pressed her lips tight and turned her head away.

With a low growl, he scooped her up into his arms and carried her into the bedroom, tossing her down on the bed. When he crawled on top of her and caught her hands above her head, Charlie was ready to admit that he was right. "Okay, okay, I give up." She gave him a quick kiss and then struggled to crawl out from underneath him. "We need to go now."

Ronan leapt up from the bed. "Let's do it."

They held hands as they hurried out to Charlotte's SUV. He helped her inside, then followed her directions as they drove through town. The theatre was housed in an old stone building that had once been the Sibleyville High School. Now it served as a community center and museum with the village offices located on the first floor.

Ronan parked the SUV and they walked inside together. The smell of the place brought back so many memories for Charlie. She'd appeared in every high school and community production from the time she'd been thirteen and knew the stage as well as she knew the oyster beds on Mistry Bay.

As she walked down the aisle, Lettie caught sight of her and clapped her hands. "Ladies and gentlemen, please welcome our new Moira Quinn, our very own Broadway star, Miss Charlotte Sibley."

The people in the theatre erupted in applause and Charlie felt a blush warm her cheeks. Ronan gave her hand a squeeze and then let go, taking a seat near the middle of the auditorium. Charlie continued down he stairs until she was standing next to Lettie.

"Remember your promise," she warned the older woman.

"You know most of the cast. Maxine Forman will be playing Bridie, your mother."

Charlie smiled at Maxine, who usually manned the front desk at the visitor's center.

"And we have a very special surprise for you. We have a new Edward, too."

Charlie watched as a familiar figure stepped out of the crowd. Her heart stopped and she sucked in a sharp breath.

"Hello, Charlie," he said.

"Danny. I'm surprised to see you back in town."

"Oh, I'm just visiting. Doing Lettie a favor. How are you?"

Charlie's heart was slamming so hard, she wasn't sure she could draw another breath to speak. What was Danny Merrick doing back in town? She hadn't seen him in more than a year, hadn't spoken to him in all that time. And suddenly, he just turns up? She glanced over at Lettie, wondering if this was all part of some master scheme.

"I'm doing really well," she said. "Great, in fact."

"You're working for your father?"

"Yes, I am." She heard the hint of defensiveness in her voice and she fought the urge to turn and run. She didn't need to explain any of her decisions to Danny. He wasn't a part of her life anymore.

"Well, I know that Sally has missed you. You remember Sally Franklin, our agent, don't you?"

"Of course I do," she muttered. What kind of game was he playing? Or more accurately, what kind of part was he playing, Charlie wondered.

"She told me that she's had a couple of calls for you but when she tried to contact you about the auditions, you never returned her call. One of them was for a nice spot on a primetime show."

"I'm not an actress anymore, Danny," she said.

"And yet, here you are. Back to doing what you do best."

Charlie wanted to turn around and walk out of the theatre. She suspected that Danny was all part of the push to get her back on the stage again, even if it was in some silly, homegrown melodrama. She glanced over her shoulder at Ronan and he smiled at her, unaware of the conversation taking place on stage.

"Let's just get started," Charlie said. "I have an early day tomorrow and I need to get out of here as fast as I can."

Danny stepped over to her and placed his hand on the small of her back. "Come with me. I'll go over the blocking with you and we can run through our lines real quick." He steered her up onto the stage and they walked over to a table with chairs around it. "You look good, Charlie. Better than good."

"Danny, I'm here as a favor to Lettie. Had I known you'd be playing opposite me, I would have refused the part. But it looks like it's a little late for that. So I'm sure you'll agree that we'll be as professional as possible and just do the job we were hired to do." She studied him shrewdly. "So how much are you getting paid for this?"

"Two thousand," he said. "I was stunned at first. I just got the call a few days ago. Lettie said something about her leading man getting arrested? I guess the mayor was going to play the role but then just dropped out. Very strange. How much did they offer you?"

"Same," she lied.

"I knew you couldn't stay away. It's in your blood, Charlie. You belong in New York, on the stage. It's your career."

Charlie cursed beneath her breath. "What career? I didn't have a career, Danny. I had a series of small jobs that didn't even come close to paying the bills."

"I just read for a big part in a soap," he said. "I should find out about that next week. If it happens, I'm going to be heading out to the west coast."

"That's wonderful."

They started with a scene between Edward and his father and Charlie sat down at the table and copied the stage directions out of the stage manager's script and into her own. As she watched her ex-boyfriend, she couldn't help but compare him to the current man in her life.

It was only now, with distance and time between them that she could see Danny's obvious flaws. What she used to take as confidence now seemed like arrogance. And his preoccupation with his looks, the constant messing with his hair or checking his image in any reflective surface now made him appear shallow and vapid instead of simply cool. And the silly acting affectations, the way he talked about "his craft" was enough to drive her right up a wall.

How had she missed all this? Had it simply gotten worse since she'd left New York or had he always been a jerk? She turned her attention back to the script, but it was impossible to study her lines. Instead, her thoughts kept jumping to the guy waiting for her in the audience.

Unlike Danny, Ronan was a real man, one who didn't pretend to be something that he wasn't. A man completely comfortable in his own skin. The thought that she'd given so much of her life to someone she could barely tolerate now was…embarrassing. And humiliating.

But Charlie still had to wonder whether there were other motives for bringing Danny back to Sibleyville. The more she thought about the possibility, the more confusing it became. Did they expect her to fall in love with him all over again, just like some silly schoolgirl? Or was the opposite supposed to happen? Was she supposed to find Ronan a much superior choice.

She turned her attention back to the script. She had three days to memorize her lines and a few more to figure the whole thing out. But the first thing she'd need to work out is how to tell Ronan that her old boyfriend was back in town. If Charlie knew anything, she knew that no one in Sibleyville was going to keep *that* a secret.

REHEARSAL LASTED LONGER than Ronan anticipated, but the time seemed to fly by. He'd never really thought about Charlie's career as an actress. Though they'd talked about her time in New York, it had never seemed real to him. But watching her move around the stage, inhabiting a completely different character than her own, was endlessly fascinating to him.

She spoke with a realistic Irish accent. Living with his grandfather for all those years, he knew what an Irish person was supposed to sound like. But more than anything, she managed to make Lettie's clumsy dialogue sound interesting.

The majority of the cast was dismissed after the first hour and Lettie worked with Charlie and the other lead for a hour longer. Ronan had been watching the male actor all evening, noticing how he reacted to Charlie, how he touched her, how he looked directly into her eyes when he spoke to her.

For an amateur actor, he wasn't bad. A little overblown in a few scenes, but he and Charlie seemed to make a good team, which was a relief considering all of Charlie's doubts about the play. Between the two of them, the story was almost believable.

When rehearsal ended, he watched as Charlie made her way up the aisle, smiling at him.

"Hey, Charlie, wait up!"

She glanced over her shoulder at her fellow actor, then quickened her pace. As she passed him, she reached out and grabbed his arm. "Come on, let's get out of here."

Ronan looked back and forth between Charlie and the guy standing on the stage, then followed Charlie out of the auditorium. "He was asking you to wait," Ronan said.

"I know. I didn't want to."

He'd never known Charlie to be impolite. "Okay," he said.

When they reached the parking lot, he slipped his arm around her waist and pulled her into a kiss. "You were really good."

"Thank you," she murmured.

"I'm not just saying that. You made the play better than it deserved to be. And your Irish accent was spot on. My grandfather would agree."

"I should quit," Charlie muttered. "I can't believe Lettie did this."

"Did what?"

She drew a deep breath and turned to him. "The guy playing opposite me is Danny Merrick. She convinced him to come back from New York to appear in her play. In fact, she paid him two thousand dollars to do it."

Ronan wasn't sure what to do with that revelation. She'd talked so little about her previous relationship that it never seemed like it would be an issue in theirs. Considering the ex was all the way in New York City, Ronan had simply put Danny Merrick out of his thoughts. But now, the guy was in town, spending time with Charlie, touching her—and at some point kissing her.

"Say something," Charlie prodded.

"Well, that's a surprise." He opened the door to the SUV for her and she hopped inside. When he got behind the wheel, she was staring at him, a perplexed expression on her face. "It is a surprise."

"That's all you have to say?" she asked.

"He's a pretty good actor, too," Ronan added. He started the vehicle and pulled out of the parking lot. "What do you want me to say?"

"I just thought you'd be more…upset. I'm furious. It's like Lettie tricked me. She knew I'd never agree to work with him. And she's even *paying* him. Like she honestly believes that I'd just let him breeze back into my life as though nothing had happened."

Ronan really was at a loss. He knew he ought to act jealous, but it was hard to work up any anger against a guy that Charlie so obviously detested. "Okay. I am angry."

"Good. Why?"

"Because you are," he said, knowing that he'd have to tread carefully. "Why are you angry?"

"I don't know," she said. "I just feel like something is going on here and I'm stuck in the middle of it." She cursed softly. "I really don't need him telling me that I ought to go back to New York and resurrect my pitiful career."

Ronan frowned. "He wants you to go back to New York? With him?"

"Yes. I would assume with him. He said that my

agent had a few job offers for me. She's left me a few voicemails, but I haven't returned her calls."

Suddenly, the anger that Ronan thought he ought to feel was beginning to bubble up inside him. "You're not going to go back, are you?"

"No!" she said. "Of course not. I'm curious as to what she found for me. I mean, it's kind of ironic that the moment I leave New York people want to hire me." She drew a deep breath. "If he sticks his tongue in my mouth when he kisses me, I'm going to kill him."

"I could probably take care of that for you," Ronan said.

Charlie laughed. "Will you help me with my lines? I have to get these memorized before tomorrow night. The play is only thirty minutes long, but I should at least give it my best effort. Not that Lettie deserves my best effort, but there probably will be a few people in the audience."

Charlie's cell phone buzzed and she pulled it out of her pocket. Ronan glanced over at her to see a look of unease cross her face. "Who is it?"

"Danny," she said. "He must have gotten my phone number from Lettie. He wants to have a drink. So that we can discuss the play." She groaned. "Oh, my God. I'm going to go crazy here."

"Do you want to talk to him?"

"I have plenty to say to him, but no, I don't want to talk to him. You know what I'd like to do. I'd like to go get a drink. You and me. I need something to relax me or I'll never get any sleep."

Ronan could think of a few things that would relax

her just fine, but obviously she wasn't looking in that direction. "Where do you want to go?"

"Windjammer," she said.

Ronan knew the place. It was just a few blocks from the boathouse. "Why don't we leave the SUV at the boathouse and walk over there. Then we can both have a drink if we want to."

By the time they reached the bar, Charlie's temper had faded and she seemed resigned to whatever Lettie had in store for her. But Ronan wasn't feeling as charitable. He knew how difficult the next few days were going to be for her, balancing work and play practice, all while seeing her ex-lover.

They found a booth in the corner and Ronan went to the bar and ordered them a couple of beers. He also placed an order for two cheeseburgers and a basket of fries.

"I ordered us something to eat," he said when he returned to the table.

"I think I know what Lettie is up to," Charlie said.

He took a sip of his beer. "What?"

"She's not trying to manipulate me. She's trying to manipulate you! She's trying to make you jealous. She thinks if she throws Danny back into my life that you'll get all possessive and declare your undying love for me."

Ronan couldn't help but wonder it Lettie's plan was already working. He didn't really like the fact that she'd be spending so much time with Danny Merrick. And the guy's appearance had managed to remind him that his feelings for Charlie were getting deeper by the day.

He stared across the table at her, at the two spots of color on her cheeks and the flicker of anger in her eyes. She was the most beautiful woman he'd ever known. And his main worry was the Danny Merrick would recognize that fact and want her back.

8

THE CENTENNIAL CELEBRATION began at noon on Friday with a parade featuring the high school band, all the fire trucks in town and the local scout troops. Charlie had given everyone Friday afternoon off so that they could enjoy the festivities, as long as they took a shift at the Mistry Bay booth at the park.

Everyone had closed up shop for the celebration, the local businesses setting up in small booths in the village park. All weekend long, Sibleyville was ready to show visitors what a great place it was to raise a family. Unfortunately, it wasn't such a great place to fall in love. But the town officials kept that minor problem to themselves.

Charlie and Ronan sat on the curb and watched as the parade marched by. Mistry Bay Oyster Farm had a small float and her younger brother and sister were seated in a huge fiberglass oyster shell, tossing candy to the children along the route.

When Charlie's youngest siblings, Garrett and Libby, saw them, they stood up and hurled candy in their direction, causing a frantic scramble around their feet. Ronan laughed, helping the children get every last piece before they scurried off, looking for more.

"This is really great," he said. "It's exactly what I imagined smalltown life to be."

"I love it, too," she said. "I remember things like this from my childhood. It was the perfect place to grow up."

When she thought about raising a family of her own, she'd always pictured it happening in Sibleyville. But as she watched the parade, she realized that other people might have had the same dream, only to leave Sibleyville to find love.

Maybe it was a self-fulfilling prophecy. Or maybe the curse was real. But the simple fact was that people didn't fall in love in Sibleyville. They were forced to look for love elsewhere all because of a tragic love story so many years ago.

She wrapped her hands around Ronan's arm and leaned against him. If the curse was true, then why was she falling in love with Ronan? He was living in Sibleyville. For now, he was a resident. She stifled a groan. Maybe it was true. Maybe they were meant to break the curse.

A horse-drawn carriage passed by with Sibleyville's mayor and his wife waving from the shiny leather seats. The Ladies' Aid Society from the local Episcopal church followed, dressed as the founding mothers, carrying brooms and butter churns and knitting needles. Charlie waved at her mother as she passed and Penny Sibley threw her a kiss.

Her father marched by as part of the local veteran's

drum core, handling the cymbals as they pounded out a cadence. Ethan was carrying the state flag in front of them, dressed in his Eagle Scout uniform.

A lone police car signaled the end of the parade. Ronan helped her up from the curb. "What's next?"

"We walk down to the park for lunch," she said. "We have a booth that sells my mom's oyster stew. She's been cooking all week over at the church kitchen."

"I love oyster stew," he said. "Let's go get some lunch."

As they walked through the crowd, Charlie was surprised at how many people greeted Ronan. Over the course of the past three and a half weeks, he'd managed to become a bit of a celebrity around town—a real Quinn in their midst.

He bought her a lemonade and they strolled through the long aisle of games—ring toss and bottle knockdown and balloon pop. Charlie introduced Ronan to a few of her friends from high school and while they were chatting, Garrett rushed up and lured Ronan away with a plan to win a new iPod at one of the ring toss games.

A few minutes later, she felt a hand on the small of her back and she turned, expecting to see Ronan. But Danny stood behind her, a charming smile on his face.

"Hey there," he said. "I was hoping I'd run into you."

Charlie groaned. "Oh, go away, Danny. Just leave me alone."

"Come on, Charlie. Don't be such a drag. We can at least be civil to each other. We were in love once, weren't we?"

"Were we?" she asked. "I'm not so sure anymore. I

think we thought we were in love, but we weren't old enough to know what that really was." She paused. "We were great friends, for awhile. And we were lovers. But we weren't in love. I know that now."

"I miss you, Charlie. It's been a year and I still think about you every day. New York isn't the same without you."

"I'm sure you've made new friends," she said.

"But I like my old friends better."

He reached out and grabbed her hand, but she snatched it away. "I need to go."

"Just wait. Give me a few minutes. I have a proposal for you."

Charlie sighed softly, running her hand through her hair. "What?"

"I want you to come back to New York. We'll be friends. You can stay at the apartment and get your career going again. I really think there are big things on the horizon for you, Charlie."

"Charlie?"

She looked to see Ronan approaching. He was carrying a plastic bag with a goldfish in it. She felt a wave of relief wash over her. He looked so sweet, his dark hair tousled by the breeze, his skin burnished brown by his days on the water. He'd never looked more handsome than at that moment.

"Hi," she said. "Who's your friend?"

He held the bag up. "Garrett won him. Or her." He chuckled. "He didn't want to carry the fish around, so I said I'd hang on to…it." He looked at Danny, then held out his hand. "Hi. We haven't met yet. I'm Ronan Quinn."

Danny blinked in surprise. "You're the Quinn?" His face turned a strange shade of grey. "You were at the theatre the other night."

"Yeah," Ronan said. "Hey, I think you're a great actor. I can really believe you're Edward Sibley."

"Thanks," Danny said. "It's not the greatest part in the world, but it's for a good cause. And I hadn't seen my folks for awhile, so I thought, what the hell."

"And you hadn't seen Charlie for a long time, either," Ronan said.

"No," Danny said. "I hadn't. So, I heard you're working for Charlie."

"Can we stop acting like I'm not even here?" Charlie said. "Yes, Ronan works for the oyster farm. He also lives with me. We're a couple. In a relationship. Together. Any other questions?"

"So, are we boyfriend and girlfriend?" Ronan asked.

"No!" Charlie said. "I mean, yes. You're not supposed to ask the questions. I was talking to Danny."

Ronan grinned. "Sorry."

"Danny, I'll see you later tonight. Ronan, I think we need to get some lunch."

She grabbed Ronan's hand and pulled him along until they'd put some distance between themselves and Danny. "Ugh, I can't believe I ever thought I was in love with him. He's just so full of himself."

"I thought he was okay," Ronan said.

She turned to him, her mouth agape, then saw the teasing glint in his eyes. "Funny." She slapped his shoulder playfully. "You are such a comedian. You're so funny, I forgot to laugh."

"Can we just clear something up here?" Ronan asked. "Are we boyfriend and girlfriend?"

"No," she said. "We're more than that. We're…together. 'Boyfriend and girlfriend' sounds so juvenile. I don't know how to express it any better."

"And you like me more than you like Danny, right?"

She laughed again. "Yes. A ton more. A bazillion times more."

"And when you kiss him tonight at the end of the play, you're going to be thinking of me?"

"Absolutely."

He bent close and brushed a kiss across her lips. "All right. I'm cool. But I want to let you know, if he picks a fight over you, I have no problem beating the shit out of him."

A laugh burst from her lips and she pushed up on her toes and kissed him again. "I'll keep that in mind. I didn't realize you were such a scrappy guy."

"There are lots of things I haven't revealed about myself yet. I'm a man of mystery."

"You are a man who makes me smile even when I feel like tearing my hair out. That's much more important."

He handed her the goldfish. "Here. You can carry this. We're going to get some of your mom's oyster stew and then we'll go home and practice your lines. I'm thinking I could offer you a few tips on that kissing scene."

"I think I could use the help," Charlie said.

As they walked toward the Mistry Bay booth, Charlie laced her fingers through his. There was no doubt about it now. She'd fallen in love with Ronan Quinn. Against all odds, he'd arrived in Sibleyville and found her.

Somehow, there had to be more at work here than just a strange coincidence. Whether it was fate or karma or destiny, some power greater than luck had put him in her path. But was she ready to ask him to stay?

THE AUDITORIUM WAS filled to the rafters for the world premiere of Leticia Trowbridge's new play, "The Curse of Bridie Quinn." Charlie had reserved a block of seats for her family, but Ronan had been too nervous to sit and instead, had found a place to pace near the back.

After a lunch of oyster stew, he and Charlie had gone back to the apartment and spent the afternoon running her lines and talking through the staging. She'd left at four for a dress rehearsal and Ronan had decided to stay behind, knowing that watching her with Danny would probably be an unnecessary annoyance.

As the lights came down and the curtain opened, he found a place to stand near the doorway. As Charlie performed, he found himself reciting her lines with her. In truth, he was probably more nervous for her than Charlie was for herself. He wasn't quite sure why that was and it seemed to defy logic. But Ronan decided that it must have something to do with his feelings about her.

Maybe when a person was in love, the connection was so deep that they could feel each other's emotions, they could sense each other's insecurities and fears. Like experiencing sympathetic stage fright.

As the play was coming to a close and Charlie was reciting her last lines, Ronan felt himself relax a bit. They still had the kiss, but he was well aware of Charlie's abilities in that area. A girl didn't forget how to kiss no matter how nervous she might be.

But when the kiss did come, Ronan wasn't prepared for the audience reaction. Though a few people clapped, the rest of the audience reacted with absolute silence followed by a low murmur of dissatisfaction.

When it came time for the curtain calls, the cast members stepped forward one by one. He noticed that they clapped the loudest for Charlie and when the mayor stepped out on stage, he gave her, Maxine and Lettie each a bouquet of roses. But the mayor had more on his mind that just congratulations. He motioned for the crowd to quiet and when they did, he cleared his throat.

"Ladies and gentlemen, I'm happy to see so many of our townsfolk come out to see this wonderful little play, written by our own Leticia Trowbridge. But we have some serious business to do here tonight. As mayor of Sibleyville, I have been authorized to sanction a marriage. A marriage that I hope will put an end, once and for all, to Bridie's curse."

Ronan felt his stomach twist. Where was this going? Were they going to make Charlie stand up on the stage while they put her through yet another plea?

"Ronan Quinn!" the mayor shouted. "Are you in the house tonight!"

Ronan raised his hand and walked halfway down the right aisle. "I am," he called.

"Good," the mayor said. "Then we have both parties here. Now, I know we've made several offers to you two over the past week, but we are prepared to sweeten the deal." He withdrew a paper from his pocket and opened his mouth to speak.

But Charlie grabbed his arm, then whispered something to him before he could continue. He frowned. "Well, just let me finish the proposal before you refuse, Charlotte. You owe us at least that much."

"We have a contract here that we're willing to offer to you and Ronan. We'd like you to consider marriage in the hopes that it might finally serve to put aside the differences between the Sibleys and the Quinns and make Sibleyville whole again. I've been authorized to offer you fifty thousand dollars, which you can split anyway you choose, for one year of marriage."

The audience erupted in wild applause and shouts of "do it, Charlie!" and "marry him!" The mayor motioned for everyone to be quiet, then peered out into the audience at Ronan. "Mr. Quinn, what do you think?"

Ronan looked at the stricken expression on Charlie's face. She looked like she wanted to find the nearest hole and crawl inside. He slowly walked down the aisle, his gaze fixed on her face. The time had come for him to make his intentions clear. He knew what he wanted and there was no use putting it off any longer.

"I would love to marry Charlotte Sibley," he said, "if she'll have me."

Charlie gasped, staring at him as if he'd just sprouted horns. "What?"

"I'm asking you to marry me, Charlie," Ronan said.

"Wait a second," Danny said. "Just wait one second. Who says we need a Quinn in order to break this curse? Both Charlotte and I are residents of Sibleyville. I want to marry her. I think we could break the curse."

This caused a major rumble in the crowd, but Ronan didn't take his eyes off of Charlie. He took a step closer. "What's it going to be?" he asked, speaking directly to her. "Are you going to marry me, Charlotte Sibley?"

"Marry me, Charlie," Danny said.

"Well now, this is an unexpected turn," the mayor said. "Perhaps we should put this to a vote. Let's have a show of hands. How many people think Charlotte should marry the Quinn?"

"Stop!" Charlie cried. "Stop this. I'm not going to let the citizens of Sibleyville determine my future. I'm the one who'll make those decisions."

"All right," the mayor said. "What is your decision? Is it going to be Danny Merrick or Ronan Quinn?"

She slowly shook her head, her eyes filling with tears. "Neither one," she said, her voice wavering with emotion. "If you want the curse to end, just stop believing it. It's as simple as that. There is no curse if you don't believe there is."

With that, she turned and ran off the stage. Ronan saw her mother, seated in the front row, get up and make her way to one of the side exits along with her brother Isaac and sister, Abby. Ronan strode up the aisle to the theatre lobby, avoiding the encouraging words from the crowd. He ran to the front doors and stepped out into the warm September night, searching the street for Charlie.

He caught sight of a figure running down the darkened sidewalk and took off after her. He was sure it was Charlie when he found the apron from her costume tossed over a hedge.

"Charlie!" he called, his voice echoing in the night air.

The streets were strangely quiet. Most of the population had been in attendance at the play. But the shadows between the streetlights made it easy for her to elude him. There was only one place she could be going. Ronan decided to head back to the boathouse.

Though he understood her reaction, Ronan wanted to make it very clear that his proposal had nothing to do with the mayor's offer. He didn't care about the money or the curse. All he cared about was having a future with Charlie. And though his proposal was somewhat unconventional, it had come from his heart.

He knew all the reasons against making a commitment like that. They'd only known each other little more than three weeks. He was supposed to return to Seattle at the beginning of next month. They hadn't even decided they were in love yet.

But nothing about their relationship had ever been normal. So maybe the proposal had come at an odd time. That didn't make it any less valid. Ronan wanted her in his life, permanently. He didn't care where they lived or what he had to do to make a living. Whatever it was, he'd make it work.

Now, he'd just have to convince her that the feelings he had for her were strong enough to withstand any doubts she had.

CHARLIE STRODE THROUGH the boathouse, tearing at the costume as she hurried up the stairs. When she got inside the apartment, she tossed it aside, piece by piece, desperate to rid herself of any reminder of the night.

She glanced around the bedroom, unable to decide what she ought to do next. She couldn't stay here. But after being humiliated in front of the entire town, where was she supposed to go?

How could he have done this to her? She'd trusted him, believed in him. And then, without a word, he'd taken their side. Did he actually think she'd believe in his marriage proposal? Sure, maybe he was trying to save her some embarrassment, but pretending to want to marry her only made things worse.

Now, when it didn't happen, everyone would feel sorry for her, the same way they did when she came home from New York. She needed to get away, just a few days, to figure out her next move. She didn't have to be back to work until Monday morning. That gave her enough time to put some distance between her and Sibleyville…and Ronan.

"Charlie?"

Ronan's voice echoed through the boathouse. Charlie quickly grabbed a pair of jeans and tugged them on, then slipped into a T-shirt she'd left draped over the end of a chair. She found her bag in the closet and tossed it onto the bed.

"Charlie?"

He was closer, in the apartment now. She pulled some clothes from her closet and tucked them into the bag. Underwear followed, along with a sweater in case it was cold wherever she was going.

"Hey."

She glanced over her shoulder to find Ronan standing in the doorway. "Hey," she said.

"What are you doing?"

"I'm getting out of town," she said. "I can't stay here."

He took a step toward her but she held out her hand. "Don't. Just don't say anything."

"Are you angry at me?"

She spun around. "Why would you do that to me? Why would you take their side? Things were so good between us and then you had to ruin it all."

"How did I ruin it?" Ronan asked.

"With that ridiculous proposal. I don't need you to ride in on your white horse and save this town. And I don't need you to rescue me from an angry mob of townsfolk. They created this problem themselves. And they keep on perpetuating it. Like tonight. If I don't marry you, then everyone there will be convinced that the curse will go on." She screamed, pressing her hands to her temples. "And there isn't even a curse!"

"I proposed because I thought it would be the best way to ensure that we'd spend the rest of our lives together."

She stared at him a long moment, then shook her head. "I have no idea what you just said."

"I want to be with you," Ronan said. "For a long time. Forever."

"You barely know me."

"I know enough. I don't think I'm going to change my mind if I take more time. I'm in love with you now. So, I think we need to move on to the next step."

"You're crazy," she said. "I'm not going to marry someone I've only known for three weeks."

"But you'd marry someone you loved?" Ronan asked.

"Yes. Of course I would."

He reached out and caught her arms, forcing her to face him. When she looked away, Ronan tipped her chin up until she met his gaze. "How do you feel about me, Charlie? Be honest. In the deepest part of your soul, how do you feel?"

She opened her mouth, then snapped it shut, shaking her head. "I don't know." She pulled away from him and returned to her packing.

"I don't believe that. I think you do know. And I think you've been trying to rationalize it in your head but you can't. It's strange and scary and real, so real that you can't bring yourself to admit it. You're in love with me the same way I'm in love with you."

"If the curse is real, then that's impossible. Two people can't fall in love in Sibleyville. And if the curse isn't real, then you don't need to marry me." She picked up the bag from the bed and carried it into the bathroom, then began to dump her toiletries into it. "Problem solved."

"Where are you going?" Ronan asked.

"I don't know. But I need you to stay here and help

out on the farm. You know how things run. Uncle Jake will help you."

He grabbed her wrist and drew her toward him. But she pulled out of his grasp. "Please, don't. We'll talk when I get back. I promise. I just have to get out of here for a little while." She pushed up on her toes and kissed his cheek. "Let my folks know that I'm all right. Tell them that I'll call them."

"All right," he said. "But I want you to call me when you get where you're going."

She nodded. "I will."

He pressed his forehead to hers and Charlie choked back another surge of tears. She wanted to stay, to crawl into bed with Ronan and make love to him until she couldn't remember anything that had happened that day.

"I'll be waiting, Charlie. I'm not going anywhere, I promise."

Drawing a deep breath, she turned and walked out of the bedroom, heading to the front door. She wanted to look back at him, just once, just to reassure herself that everything he said was true. "Thank you," she murmured, refusing to face him. "I appreciate what you tried to do."

"I know," Ronan said.

She walked out the door, then hurried down the steps to the ground floor of the boathouse. When she got inside, she hopped into the SUV and turned the key. The engine roared to life. She threw the vehicle into gear and pointed it north, away from the celebration, away from the place of her humiliation.

It was only after she'd left the town limits that she

allowed herself to think about what Ronan had said to her. He loved her. And he wanted to stay with her. She ought to be jumping for joy, shouting to the rooftops, that she'd finally found the perfect man.

But she'd always expected that when her perfect man came along, she'd be perfectly certain that she was in love too. And right now, she wasn't certain about anything.

9

RONAN HAD WORKED until his muscles ached, until sweat poured out of his body and until he was so exhausted he could barely stand. It was the only way he could sleep.

Charlie had been gone for five days and he hadn't heard a word from her. He didn't know where she was or who she was with, but he'd convinced himself that as long as he stayed in Sibleyville, she'd come back to him.

Still, lying alone in bed, he'd had his doubts. Maybe she'd gone back to New York, back to the man she'd once loved. He'd seen her mother at the office and she'd assured him that the moment Charlie called, he'd be the first to know. But Penny Sibley didn't seem nearly as concerned as Ronan was.

As for the rest of the folks in Sibleyville, the gossip had been running wild. They knew that Charlie had left town and many of them had made it a point to thank Ronan for his efforts in ending the curse, even though it didn't look like a marriage was in the cards.

Ronan carefully steered the skiff into its spot along the dock, then grabbed the lines and fastened them around the cleats. He and Jack had worked together that afternoon, harvesting oysters from the west shore of Mistry Bay. They'd worked quickly, but silently, neither one of them interested in idle conversation.

He tucked the thermos under his arm and picked up the small cooler that had held his lunch, then jumped onto the dock. But as he climbed the steps up to the street, he noticed a figure at the top. Danny Merrick had left town right after the play and now he was back.

"What do you want?" Ronan asked.

"I need to talk to Charlie. Do you know where she is?"

Ronan shook his head. Even if he did know, he wasn't about to tell this guy. "I thought she was in New York," he muttered.

"Is she?"

"I don't know. I haven't heard from her."

"She's not in New York," Danny said.

"Well, then, why don't you just give me a message and if I see her, I'll try to remember to give it to her." He yanked open the front door of the boathouse and walked inside, ignoring the man who hurried in behind him.

Ronan kicked off his boots, then slipped out of the waders. "Well?"

"She needs to come back to New York. Not for me, but for her career. I know I made things impossible for her there, but she has an amazing talent and I don't want to see her waste her life harvesting oysters and growing old in this pathetic little town."

"Is that all?" Ronan asked.

"No. Tell her that her agent has been trying to reach

her. She's got an audition for a new television series next week. It's an important job. She should at least give it a shot."

"All right. Great. I'll tell her all that."

Danny gave him a suspicious look. "You think you know what's best for her?"

Ronan shook his head. "Nope. I want her to be happy. That's all I care about."

"And what if she decides she wants to be happy with me?"

"I don't think that will happen. But, if it does, then I'll wish her the best. And I'll also probably put an Irish curse on your career. I'm a Quinn. I can do that, you know."

For a moment, he thought Danny just might challenge him. He clenched his fists at his sides and his face turned red. "It was nice meeting you," he muttered. "When you see Charlie, tell her I'm sorry."

Ronan reached for the front door and held it open. Danny walked through and he let it swing shut behind him. He strode through the boathouse, then took the stairs two at a time. When he reached the second story, he found Mrs. Sibley at her desk, piles of receipts scattered around her.

"Ronan, how are you?"

"I'm fine," he said. "How about you?"

She smiled. "You don't look fine. You look exhausted."

"I am. But the hard work helps me sleep at night."

"Well, Jake says you're doing a wonderful job. He's hoping you'll stay on with us. And don't think we don't appreciate what you're doing, covering for Charlie while she's gone."

Ronan shrugged. "I don't mind. I enjoy the work."

Penny glanced up from her receipts, then pulled her reading glasses off. "She's not going to like that I told you, but she came home late last night."

A sigh of relief came out in a rush. "She's all right?"

Penny nodded. "She's fine. A little confused, perhaps. A bit embarrassed for running away in the first place. But I'm sure she'll work everything out in time."

"Thanks for letting me know," he said.

"Well, I was thinking you might like to come for dinner tonight. Nothing fancy. Or foreign. Meat loaf and mashed potatoes. Charlie is cooking. Maybe you'll have a chance to talk."

Ronan had thought a lot about what he would say to Charlie when he saw her again. But now that he had the chance, he was riddled with indecision. "Do you think she'd be okay with that?"

"We won't know until you try," Penny replied. "Get yourself cleaned up and see how you feel. We eat at six."

Ronan considered his options for a long moment. He'd missed her. He'd missed having her with him all day long. And he'd missed sleeping beside her at night. When a guy loved a girl, they were supposed to be together. The sooner he made that happen again, the better.

"I think I will take you up on that invitation," Ronan said. "Maybe I can start to repair some of the damage I've done."

"Oh, sweetheart, you haven't done any damage at

all. All you've done is make Charlie happy. There's no fault in that. If you do love her like you say you do, then nothing needs to be fixed. You just keep telling her how you feel and one day, she'll look at you and she'll believe you."

"All right. Well, I'm going to get ready."

"Wear that blue shirt," she said. "It brings out the color of your eyes."

Ronan grinned. "Okay. Thanks for the advice."

He wandered back to the apartment and when he closed the door behind him, he leaned back against it. He might only get one chance to make things right with her.

He hadn't had much experience wooing women. Hell, he'd never had to work hard to get women interested in being with him. When it came to flowers and candy and dating, he was at a loss.

Did all women like flowers? He knew Charlie wasn't a big fan of chocolate, but she loved gummy worms. But a bag of gummy worms didn't seem like a proper peace offering. There was always jewelry, but jewelry could sometimes be misinterpreted. A necklace didn't mean as much as a ring. And where did earrings fall into the mix?

Ronan groaned. Though he'd never solicited advice from his brothers regarding women, right now, he could actually use some. Between Cameron, Dermot and Kieran, at least one of them would know how to handle his dinner with Charlie.

He was on his own. And at this point, he knew a box of chocolates or a blue shirt or a diamond ring wasn't going to convince Charlie to fall in love with him. He'd have to find a way to show her that there wasn't a man in the world who'd ever love her as much as he did.

He'd stay in Sibleyville until that happened. If it took a year or even two, he was willing to show her that he wasn't going to cut and run. "Be prepared, Charlotte Sibley," he murmured to himself. "I've found a new life and it's not going to officially start unless you're a part of it."

CHARLIE BRUSHED A strand of hair from her face as she kneaded the dough for biscuits. Grabbing a handful of flour, she sprinkled it on the counter, then worked the dough into a neat square.

"Why are you making biscuits when we're having potatos?" Abby asked. "Double starch. That's kind of redundant."

The truth was Charlie didn't know why she was making biscuits. It was one of the only things she did well when it came to baking. And right now, she was looking for anything to take her mind off of Ronan. If she knew how to knit, she'd be making mittens. "I want biscuits," she said.

Charlie had arrived back home late last night from a five-day trip to Bar Harbor. She'd hoped to take long walks around town to clear her head. But instead, she found herself wishing that Ronan had come with her and that they could enjoy the fall weather together.

Depressed and lonely, she shut herself in her motel room and watched movies all day long. After running up a hundred dollar pay-per-view bill, she checked out and decided she could watch movies at home for free.

It felt safe here in familiar surroundings. She hadn't ventured out yet, unwilling to face the concerns, unable to provide any answers to the questions. Was she in love with Ronan Quinn? Was he going to stay in Sibleyville and marry her? Or was she going to go on as she had been for the last year, another sad spinster caught by the curse.

Abby walked into the kitchen. "I'm glad you're home, Charlie."

She gave her sister a hesitant smile. "Thanks. Me, too."

"I'm sorry for what happened to you after the play. They shouldn't have done that to you. Not in front of the whole town."

"It was pretty embarrassing. I guess I always thought that when a man finally asked for my hand, it might be just a little romantic."

"But it was romantic," Abby said. "I mean, he just walked right down that aisle and told the whole town that he wanted you. He was like some modern day knight and you were his damsel in distress."

"I think what he wanted was to save me from the humiliation."

"But isn't that what a guy in love would do?" Abby asked.

"Abs, you don't fall in love in three weeks. No one does."

"Mom and Dad always taught us that we Sibleys do things in our own way, not like other people. If you fall in love in three weeks, then that's just the way it's going to be for you." She paused. "Do you love him?"

Charlie closed her eyes and drew a slow breath. "Yes. I think I do. But my practical side says that I need more time to be sure."

Abby grinned and clapped her hands. "I knew you loved him. I told Mom that night after the play. I could see it in the way you looked at him." She jumped off the counter and threw her arms around Charlie's shoulders. "I have to tell you, the man is not hard on the eyes. He is a grade A hottie. And you two will make perfectly beautiful babies together."

"Don't get ahead of yourself," Charlie said. "I don't even know if he's still in town."

"Oh, he is. He's been working with Uncle Jake. Danny left though. And came back. And then left again after Ronan threatened to put a curse on his career. I don't think we'll be seeing him in Sibleyville anytime soon."

"What's the gossip around town?"

"Everyone is really sorry. Some people are calling for the mayor and Lettie Trowbridge to make a public apology."

The front door squeaked and Charlie wiped her hands on a towel. "If that's Libby, tell her I need her to come in and unload the dishwasher. It's her turn. And if it's Garrett, have him take the garbage out to the curb."

"No prob," Abby said as she pushed open the swinging door into the dining room.

"And go find Mom," Charlie called after her. "I'm

not sure where Dad went and I need to know if she still wants to eat at six."

She didn't get an answer from Abby and figured that her sister had already raced upstairs. She found the biscuit cutter in a drawer and began to cut circles from the flattened dough, tossing the rounds onto a baking sheet.

Ronan was still in town, she mused. Maybe after dinner she'd wander down to the boathouse and check her mail. Or she could wait until later and sneak into the apartment and—

The kitchen door swung open and she looked up, prepared to give a task to one of her younger siblings. But the order stopped in her throat as she came face to face with Ronan.

Charlie stared at him for a long moment, her heart pounding in her chest, her breath coming in quick gasps. She fought the urge to run into his arms, to throw herself at him until he kissed her like he used to.

She wasn't sure how long he waited, his hands tucked in the back pockets of his jeans, his blue shirt making his sun-burnished skin look even more beautiful. But at some point, he took a step toward her. She felt a shiver skitter up her spine and her knees wobbled slightly.

"Hello," she said.

"Hi," Ronan replied. "I'm glad you're back."

"Me—me, too."

"Did you get enough of a break?"

Charlie nodded. "I think so. I didn't want to take too much time away. I drove up to Bar Harbor."

"I don't know where that is," he said. He pulled his hands out of his pockets and rubbed his palms together.

"I was going to bring you flowers, but I didn't know what kind you liked. And I've never seen you eat much candy so that was out."

"How are things at the oyster farm?" she asked, trying to change the subject.

"Good. We've hardly missed you." He paused. "Actually, we've all missed you. But we've managed without you. Not that we wanted to. Everyone will be glad that you're back."

"Thanks. I knew you'd be able to handle everything."

Another uncomfortable silence grew between them and she could see that Ronan was growing impatient with the pace of the conversation. "So I'm going to say what I came here to say," he said. "And then I'm going to leave."

He slowly walked toward her and when he was close enough to touch her, Ronan stopped. She'd been dreaming about this moment for the past five days and now that it was here, Charlie wasn't sure what she ought to do. Listening to him would be a good start.

"Before I met you, I lived in a pretty dark place. I was carrying around a lot of pretty heavy baggage and I didn't feel like I belonged anywhere. And then, you opened the door of the boathouse and it was like I walked into sunshine for the first time in my life. And it was warm and bright and I felt like I could be happy."

"Ronan, I—"

He pressed a finger to her lips. "I have to say this all at once or I'll never get it out, Charlie." He drew a deep breath. "You've changed my life. I want to stay here with you. And if you don't want to marry me, that's fine. Just working with you will be enough." He paused for a moment, then hurried on. "And if you don't want to work with me, I'll find another job."

"You would?" she asked. "You'd quit."

Ronan took her hand and stared down at her fingers as he carefully slipped them between his. "I need to be near you. You're like air and water to me. I can't live unless I have you. And I'm willing to do whatever it takes to make that happen."

"You're sure you want to stay in Sibleyville?"

"I want to be wherever you want to be. We can go live on an island somewhere, in a hut with fish and coconuts to eat and hours to lay around in the sun."

"That sounds more like a honeymoon to me."

He looked up at her, his gaze meeting hers, his eyes searching for an answer. "It could be. But we'd have to get married first."

"We've never done things the usual way in my family."

"All right, honeymoon first. We'll figure out the wedding later."

She drew his hands up and clutched them to her chest. "I think I could do that, Ronan."

For the first time since he walked in, he smiled at her. And for Charlie, it was like a door had opened up and the sun had come pouring in too. "I do love you, Ronan. I know it sounds crazy, but I don't think I can live without you either."

He pulled her into his arms and kissed her. Charlie felt her knees go weak and her pulse begin to race. Everything that she'd ever wanted in life was here in his arms. She'd never realized that her dreams didn't have to be a career or an interesting place to live, fame and fortune. She'd found her dreams in this man, this stranger who'd walked into her life and stolen her heart.

As long as they were together, life would be perfect. "Are you going to be staying for dinner?" she asked.

"I was hoping we could go back to the apartment and eat some oysters."

"And?"

"I'm happy to start with the oysters," he said. "We'll see what happens after that."

She grabbed his hand and pulled him along through the house and toward the front door. "Abby, take care of dinner. Ronan and I are leaving."

"What?" her sister cried.

The screen door slammed and a minute later, she and Ronan were running across the lawn toward her SUV. "You know, I'm thinking we're going to have to fix one thing about this relationship of ours."

"And what's that?"

"I don't think I want to be your boss anymore. I think maybe we ought to try business partners."

"Will you still boss me around in bed?" Ronan asked.

She laughed. "I think you can count on that."

Epilogue

THE FOUR QUINN brothers gathered around the table in the conference room at Quinn Yachtworks. It was New Year's Eve and a celebration had been planned for later that evening at one of Seattle's best restaurants. But for now, Martin Quinn was in charge of the festivities.

He surveyed the room, studying each of his grandsons and the women they'd brought to the party. When he'd sent them off to find a new life for themselves, he'd expected some major revelations. But he'd never expected each of them to return with fiances and in one case, a wife.

Cameron had been living in Albuquerque for the past few months, the love of his life a pretty ex-cop named Sofia Reyes. He'd split the design business away from Quinn Yachtworks and was working as a consultant rather than a business partner.

Dermot had been back in Seattle since early October and Rachel Howe, his partner, had arrived shortly after, leaving her life in Wisconsin behind for a new life with Dermot. Dermot's twin, Kieran had found love with a feisty country singer and songwriter who had been playing small venues around the Seattle area as she took a new direction in her career.

And Ronan, the grandson who'd suffered the most at the loss of his parents, had found a brand new life away from Seattle and the memories that had darkened his life for so long. He'd brought Charlotte along on his trip back to see his brothers, introducing her as his wife.

Martin had always dreamed about the day he would turn the business over to his grandsons, but he'd known that forcing them to buy into his dream had been wrong. Their grief at the loss of their parents was something he'd been unprepared to deal with. So he'd done the best he could.

And now, with their happiness assured, he'd been able to undo at least some of the damage he might have caused. Martin cleared his throat and reached for his champagne flute. "I'm sure you boys would like to get on with your celebrations, so I'm going to make this very quick."

"Cameron and Ronan. You've chosen to make a life for yourselves outside of Seattle." Martin's executive assistant, Miriam, handed them each an envelope. "This is a down payment on each of your twenty-percent shares in Quinn Yachtworks. For the next five years, you'll receive monthly payments until Kieran and Dermot have bought out your interests."

Miriam handed two larger envelopes to the twins. "You'll want to have lawyers look those over," Martin suggested. "But those papers turn control of the yachtworks over to you two. I have officially cashed in my share and will be taking half of it out in merchandise."

Cameron frowned. "Merchandise?"

"Hull number 854," Martin said. "It's being fitted right now and as soon as it's launched, your grandfather is going to sail around the world."

Dermot gasped and he turned to his brothers with a worried look on his face. "Alone? Hull 854 is a fourty-six footer. You can't take a boat that size out alone."

"I have a friend I'll be taking with me."

"Who?" Ronan asked.

"Miriam."

This time they didn't look at each other. They just stared at him in disbelief. "Miriam? Our Miriam?"

"My Miriam," Martin said, holding out his arm. Miriam smiled and stepped to his side.

"Miriam," Kieran repeated.

"Yes. We've been sailing together for many years now and we thought it was time to retire and see a little bit of the world."

"Miriam," Ronan said. "My gosh. Congratulations. And welcome to the family." He looked at his grandfather. "You are planning to marry her, aren't you?"

"We've discussed it," Miriam said.

Martin nodded. "I've already made the offer and she's thinking about it." He picked up his glass. "So, here we are. I look at you four and your lovely ladies and I think about the trip I made all those years ago. Almost fifty years now. It seems like just yesterday that I stepped off that plane carrying your father. He and your mother would be so proud to see this. So I'd like to make a toast to my favorite boys and their favorite girls. To Cam and Sofie, to Kieran and Maddie, to Dermot and Rachel, and to Ronan and Charlotte."

Rachel held up her glass. "And to Martin and Miriam."

"To Martin and Miriam," they all said.

"May you always walk in sunshine. May you never want for more. May Irish angels rest their wings right beside your door." He touched his glass to Miriam's. "Sláinte chuig na fir, agus go mairfidh na mná go deo."

"Are you going to tell us what that means?" Dermot asked.

"Health to the men and may the women live forever."

For the next half hour, the champagne flowed and laughter filled the conference room. Martin couldn't help but remember the dark days that they'd weathered after the disappearance of his son and daughter-in-law.

But he felt their presence here now, for the first time since they'd been lost. Gathered around the table, he saw Jamie's smile and Suzanne's sparkling eyes. He saw her thick dark hair and his strong profile. And someday soon, he'd look into the faces of his great-grandchildren and know that Jamie and Suzanne weren't really lost at all.

They lived on in the children of their children.

* * * * *